Rh

Revenge

A Sandy Bay Cozy Mystery

By

Amber Crewes

First published in March 2020

All characters and events in this publication, other than those clearly in the public domain, are fictitious and any resemblance to real persons, living or dead, is purely coincidental.

Copyright © Pen-n-a-Pad Publishing

For questions and comments about this book, please contact info@ambercrewes.com

ISBN: 9798620744107
Imprint: Independently Published

Other books in the Sandy Bay Series

Apple Pie and Trouble

Brownies and Dark Shadows

Cookies and Buried Secrets

Donuts and Disaster

Éclairs and Lethal Layers

A Sandy Bay

COZY MYSTERY

Book Eighteen

1

Meghan Truman grinned as the airplane began descending over Sandy Bay, her adopted hometown in the Pacific Northwest. She was exhausted from a long overnight layover in San Francisco; her eyes were red and her long dark hair was tangled, but as she spotted the town from afar as she peeked out the window, her heart pounded with excitement; she had been away from home for nearly a month, and she couldn't wait to get back to her work, friends, and fiancé.

Her fiancé. Meghan's heart fluttered as she thought of Jack Irvin, her husband-to-be. Jack had proposed to her before the holidays, and he had even flown to her hometown in Texas to spend Christmas with her family. His job as a detective for the Sandy Bay Police Department required he leave just after New Year's Day, and Meghan hadn't seen him in over a week. She looked down at her engagement ring, her eyes crinkling with joy as she remembered Jack's proposal, and she could hardly wait to see him at the airport arrivals hall.

The small regional jet gently touched down at the Sandy Bay Airport, and Meghan squirmed as the passengers around her slowly packed up their belongings; she wanted nothing more than to dash

into the arms of her handsome fiancé, and she was

bursting with impatience. Finally, it was her turn to leave, and she leapt into the aisle of the plane and marched into the airport.

Meghan glanced at her reflection in the window of a coffee shop as she made her way to the arrivals hall. "I look horrible," she lamented as she pulled a scrunchie out of her backpack and tucked her hair into a messy bun. "Thank goodness Jack and I are engaged now, otherwise, if he saw me looking this rough, he'd probably run for the hills!"

She turned a corner, passed the security station, and entered the arrivals hall. Her cheeks flushed as she spotted Jack waving at her. He had a hand behind his back, and as she approached, he pulled the hand free to reveal a bouquet of red roses.

"You shouldn't have!" Meghan exclaimed as she threw her arms around her fiancé and kissed him on the lips. "Babe, you are already getting me from the airport and taking your personal time to do it! You didn't have to bring me flowers."

Jack winked. "Only the best for my beautiful wife-to-be."

"I'm not feeling so beautiful," she told him as they

turned to walk to the baggage claim. "That overnight layover in San Francisco did a number on me; I wanted to pay for my ticket, but I really should have used my parents' frequent flier miles and flown directly last night."

Jack leaned down and gave her a peck on the cheek.

"I think you look stunning," he told her earnestly. "I've never been happier to see you."

As they waited for her bags, Meghan recounted everything that happened before she left her parents' home in Texas. Right before Christmas, her father had gotten into some legal trouble, but her parents had worked out a deal that ensured her father wouldn't be in prison forever for his white collar crime; the Trumans were incredibly wealthy, and they were able to pull some strings that allowed Henry Truman, her father, to receive a reduced sentence of three days in jail and a year of probation. This news had come the day after Christmas, and all the Trumans were delighted that Henry would be able to have a fresh start in the new year.

"Were your parents sad to see you go?" Jack asked as he lifted Meghan's suitcase from the luggage carousel. "They sure loved having us in Texas."

Meghan rolled her dark eyes. "They made such a scene at the airport," she sighed. "Mom was crying her eyes out, and Daddy was huffing and puffing about me moving to the Pacific Northwest. "Why would you want to live in a dark cloud, Meghan? You and Jack should move to Texas after the wedding. Come join my business; you know that I would love to have you in the family business, and I can put Jack to work as well."

Jack raised an eyebrow. "He said that?"

She nodded. "I know they don't think my job as the owner and operator of a bakery is glamorous enough;

Mama refuses to call it a bakery and keeps referring to it as my 'business venture'. She is so pretentious sometimes."

Jack gestured toward the exit. "My car is in the parking garage. Let's go, babe."

They left the airport and walked outside. Meghan shuddered as a gust of cold air hit her. "I think the only thing I didn't miss about Sandy Bay is the weather; it's so cold there!"

"That winter sea air is the worst," Jack agreed. He looked down at Meghan. "Babe, do you think your parents really want us to move to Texas? Would your dad really give us both jobs?"

Meghan peered up at her fiancé. "Why do you ask?"

Jack shrugged. "My job is getting more and more difficult each month," he admitted. "Being a detective is not for the faint of heart. I feel burnt out, to be honest, and living in warm Texas and working for my in-laws doesn't sound too stressful…"

Meghan cackled. "Oh honey," she laughed. "They have you *fooled*! Living in close proximity to my parents would be the most stressful job of your life!"

Jack's piercing blue eyes stared down at her. "That's not very nice to say about your parents," he chided.

She was taken aback. "Do you forget how many parties they dragged us to at Christmas while you were visiting?" she asked. "Or how many times my

daddy demanded you play golf with him? Or the craziness from all of my sisters? Imagine all of that times a thousand if we were to move to Texas. My parents are amazing, but they are also very controlling. They want to be in charge. If we live near them and work for them, they are going to call all the shots in our life together, and that is the last thing I want."

"Fair enough," Jack agreed. "I just didn't want to let a good opportunity slip away from us if you thought it would be a good idea… and clearly, you don't."

Meghan glanced up at him and batted her eyelashes. "You know what I think is a *great* idea?" she asked flirtatiously.

"What?"

"Getting married to you," she declared. "Mama and I were busy with wedding plans last week, and she almost had a conniption when I told her I don't think I want my bridesmaids to carry bouquets."

Jack shook his head. "I don't know what that even means," he laughed. "I'll let you ladies do the planning."

"Mama has completely taken over," Meghan informed him. "We don't even have a date yet, but she's already having fabrics sent to the house, holding auditions for a string quartet, and sampling cakes in town."

"She's excited we're getting married at your

childhood home, isn't she?"

"To say the least!"

They reached the car, and Jack opened the passenger door for Meghan. She climbed in and leaned back against the leather seat. She turned to Jack and blew a kiss at him as he sat down beside her. "I have never been happier to see you."

He reached over and took her hand, giving it a firm squeeze. "I've never been happier to see *you*. I missed you, Meghan, and now that you're home, I have a proposal for you."

Meghan flashed her engagement ring at him. "Sorry, Mister, but you've already given me the best proposal I could ever ask for. It's too late for another one."

Jack grinned, pushing back his blonde hair as it fell in his eyes. "How about another proposal? What do you think about getting married sooner rather than later? I know we talked about a wedding in August, but that seems so far away. I don't want to wait another eight months to make you my wife. What would you say about sneaking away and eloping? We could run off to Mexico or somewhere nice and get married by ourselves on the beach. What do you say?"

Meghan's stomach churned. "That sounds so romantic," she admitted. "But what about my parents? I know it's overwhelming trying to plan a wedding with them, but they are so excited about hosting us in Texas. They would be devastated if we canceled on them and eloped."

She noticed a twinkle in Jack's eyes. "I have a solution," he told her. "We can elope secretly."

"*Secretly*?"

He nodded. "The pair of us can steal away for a long weekend and get married. We won't tell anyone, and we can go through with the Texas wedding as planned! It might be stressful, but we'll have a private laugh about it because we'll both know we are *already* married!"

Meghan bit her lip. "That *is* tempting," she told him. "I do want to marry you as soon as possible... maybe we should look into it! What could stop us? If we don't tell anyone, my parents will never find out, and we could still go through with the big fancy wedding in Texas…"

Jack squeezed her hand again. "Just think about it," he urged her. "I think we could make some really special memories together…. you and me, on the beach, the sun setting…"

"How romantic," Meghan giggled. "Let's talk more about it later when I have gotten some shut-eye! I think it would be a fun idea and I really think we should talk it over."

They drove in peaceful silence for the rest of the way. When they pulled up in front of Truly Sweet, the bakery Meghan owned and operated, she squealed. "I have never been happier to get back to work!" she exclaimed as she threw off her seatbelt. "I hope Trudy and Pamela have been able to hold down the fort."

She skipped inside, bursting through the yellow front door. "Pamela? Trudy?"

Pamela, her sixteen-year-old employee, waved from behind the counter. "You're back!"

Meghan ran to hug her. "It's so good to see you," she told her. She stepped back and examined Pamela's face. "You look older!"

Pamela giggled. "It's only been three weeks. I can't possibly look older."

Meghan narrowed her eyes. "It's your hair," she announced. "You cut it and dyed it, didn't you? What did your mother have to say about that?"

Pamela bit her lip. "She didn't like it," she admitted as she ran her hands through her short bob. "She liked my natural color better, but she thinks I'll grow out of having this dark color."

Meghan winked. "Mothers are usually right about those things. Where is Trudy?"

"I'm here," Trudy called out from the kitchen. "Be right there."

Jack walked inside carrying Meghan's things. "Here you are, babe," he told her. "I have to run off to work, but let me give you a kiss."

He kissed her softly on the lips and she smiled. "Love you, Mr. Irvin," she breathed happily.

"Love you, Soon-to-be Mrs. Irvin," he replied as he walked out of the bakery.

"That was too adorable," Pamela gushed. "How are the wedding plans?"

Meghan thought about Jack's elopement proposal and blushed. "They're... fine," she stammered. "Tell me about you, Pamela. What's new around here?"

Pamela wrinkled her nose. "Well, Mrs. Sheridan and Frank had a nasty falling out."

"What?" Meghan cried. Mrs. Sheridan was an elderly local who had a big personality; she was always getting into others' business, and while many didn't care for her, Meghan had taken a liking to her. Mrs. Sheridan was engaged to her boyfriend, Frank, a retired doctor, and Meghan was sad to hear that they weren't getting along.

"Tell me more."

Pamela nodded. "They got into a huge fight at the skating rink; Mrs. Sheridan wanted to wear her old costume from her figure skating days, and Frank told her the skirt was too short and revealing for someone her age and that the sequins didn't flatter her. He didn't want her wearing something like that in public. He said it was tasteless."

"Yikes."

"Mrs. Sheridan started hitting him on the bottom with her cane, and the police came out. They issued her a warning, and she stormed off. She's been acting

strange ever since, and word on the street is that they still haven't reconciled."

Meghan shook her head. "Oh no. Mrs. Sheridan is something else; there is nothing that woman could do that would surprise me…"

Trudy, her middle-aged employee, marched out of the kitchen holding a hot pie. "Meghan, wait until you try this," she smiled.

Meghan inhaled. "Is that rhubarb pie?"

Pamela nodded. "When you emailed me during the holidays and mentioned that your mom made it to perfection, I wanted to give it a go. Trudy and I have been working on the recipe, and I think we have it down. Give it a try?"

Meghan nodded and retrieved a small silver fork from behind the counter. She lifted the tiny piece of the pie to her mouth and took a bite. "Pamela! Trudy! This isn't pie... this is *art*!"

Pamela grinned. "We put in a lot of work."

"What did you add to the recipe? It tastes a bit different than my mom's, but honestly, it's even better than hers!"

Trudy gestured at Pamela. "Ask her; she was the mastermind behind this."

Pamela couldn't keep the smile off of her face. "I used organic brown cane sugar instead of plain old white sugar," she began. "And I used apple sauce

instead of butter. I tried to make some adjustments so it would be vegan and gluten-free. Can you tell?"

Meghan shook her head. "Not at all; the flavor is perfect, and the rhubarb taste is unmistakable! This is fantastic, Pamela."

She wanted to continue praising the dessert, but she noticed Trudy was staring out the window.

"Trudy? What's the matter?"

Trudy's eyes widened. "Look, ladies," she pointed out the front window. "Just *look* at that! I can't believe my eyes!"

2

Meghan stifled a gasp as Sally Sheridan strutted into the bakery. Mrs. Sheridan, who typically favored cardigans and ankle-length tartan skirts, was dressed in a pink sequin mini skirt, and Meghan could not believe how pale her skinny legs were. She wore a matching long sleeve shirt, barrettes in her hair, and makeup on her face.

"What are you looking at?" Mrs. Sheridan growled as Meghan tried to regain composure.

"You look…. different today," Pamela chimed in, her eyes wide.

Mrs. Sheridan placed a hand on her hip. "What? You don't like my makeup?"

Meghan bit her lip. "It's not just the makeup," she began. "Your outfit is different than the clothes you usually wear."

Mrs. Sheridan rolled her eyes. "Different as in ALL OF THAT AND A BAG OF CHIPS? Yeah, I know. I look better than I've looked in fifteen years after all the Pilates classes I've been taking, and I want to show off a little."

Trudy's eyes were nearly bulging out of her head, and Pamela could hardly contain her laughter. Meghan took a long breath in through her nose, knowing that she had to be delicate about the way she handled this situation. "Is there a particular reason you feel like showing off?"

Mrs. Sheridan's face darkened. "I saw Frank talking to another woman at the skating rink," she muttered as a lock of her silver hair got caught on her glossy lips. She batted at it in annoyance. "She was flirting with him, and instead of walking away from her, he kept talking to her?"

Trudy raised an eyebrow. "Who was it? Did you know her?"

Mrs. Sheridan shook her head. "Haven't the slightest idea," she told them. "But if my man is going to make eyes at another woman, I'm going to dress in a way that ensures his eyes will stay on *me*. I know I look good, so I am going to flaunt what I have, ladies!"

Pamela leaned in to whisper to Meghan discreetly. "My mom would kill me if I left the house looking like that," she said. "Mrs. Sheridan looks like she took a long walk in the Red Light District in Amsterdam."

"Pamela!" Meghan gasped. "How do you know about the Red Light District?"

Pamela winked. "I may be young, but I know a thing or two, Meghan."

Meghan frowned. "You're too young to be talking about these kinds of things. Go back to the kitchen for now until Mrs. Sheridan leaves. I want you to start rolling out the dough for the cinnamon cookies."

"But…"

"No buts!" Meghan said firmly. "Go!

Pamela shot her a look, but she obediently trudged back to the kitchen. Mrs. Sheridan was now sitting on one of the little white iron tables, her legs crossed in a salacious fashion. Trudy looked alarmed as she glanced back and forth between Mrs. Sheridan and the customers sitting at a nearby table.

"Don't you think I look good?" Mrs. Sheridan crooned as Trudy's eyes widened.

"You look great," Meghan hurriedly assured her, wanting to minimize the scene Mrs. Sheridan was making in the bakery. "Why don't we all go back into the kitchen? I think we should have some snacks."

She caught Trudy's eye, and the two women nodded at each other, both knowing it was imperative to get Sally Sheridan out of the dining room and out of the view of their customers. Meghan even placed a hand on Mrs. Sheridan's shoulder to gently guide her out of the room.

They entered the kitchen, and Meghan was pleasantly surprised to find her friend and business partner, Jackie, waiting for her. "Surprise!"

Meghan grinned. "What are you doing here?"

Jackie's eyes sparkled with excitement. "I wanted to hear all about the wedding plans," she gushed as she embraced Meghan. "You said that you and your mama had started some of the planning, and as your Maid-of-Honor, I need to be in the know."

Meghan smiled weakly. She knew that Jackie was not going to be her Maid-of-Honor; she had so many sisters that she would likely just make all of them her Maids and Matrons-of-Honor, but she did not want to rile Jackie up when Mrs. Sheridan was already a loose cannon in her kitchen.

"There's not a lot to talk about," she admitted sheepishly. "We're getting married at my parents' house this August, but other than that, I don't have a lot of details."

"Am I invited?" Mrs. Sheridan interjected.

"We haven't started our guest list," Meghan said nervously. "But yes, you will be invited."

Mrs. Sheridan flipped her hair. "I should start thinking about my outfit *now*; I'm sure you'll have plenty of pretty little bridesmaids for Frank to look at, so I need to make sure my outfit for your wedding is

over the top. I am going to go shopping right now! Bye, ladies."

Meghan sighed as Mrs. Sheridan hobbled out of the bakery. "What was that about?" Jackie asked.

"You don't want to know," she replied. "Let's catch up in the dining area now that she's gone; the customers won't be staring at you."

She led Jackie out to the dining room and they sat at one of the little white tables. "What's new with you?" Meghan asked.

"Not too much," Jackie said, folding her hands. "Things are fine at the salon, and the reservations at the barn are nice and steady despite the cold weather."

Meghan smiled, happy to hear the news about the barn. She and Jackie had bought and renovated a historical barn together last year, and now, it was a popular place to hold events. The barn had seen its fair share of weddings, baby showers, family reunions, and parties, and it was a nice source of side income for both women.

"You look great," Meghan complimented. "I love that shade of violet; it really brings out your eyes."

Jackie blushed. "That's what Dan said. He said the violet hair added more spark to my look."

"Dan? Who is Dan?"

Jackie batted her eyelashes. "It's a new thing," she admitted. "It isn't serious yet, and we are taking it slow, but we've been spending a lot of time together, and I really like him."

Meghan grinned. "I'm happy to hear you're taking it slow," she told her friend. "But I haven't seen you smile like that in a long time. Dan might be a keeper!"

Jackie's cheeks turned even redder. "I hope so," she replied. "I want to find someone. I want to be happy like you and Jack. I want a wedding!"

Meghan chose not to mention that Jackie had been married before and had a wedding, so instead, she nodded politely.

"You said the wedding plans aren't finalized, but what about the other events?" Jackie asked, changing the subject to Meghan's relief.

"Other events?"

"The bridal shower, the engagement party, and the bachelorette party?"

Meghan shrugged. "I don't love attention… you know that," she stated. "I don't know if I want any of those events. I think a wedding will be enough for me."

Jackie's jaw dropped. "You're telling me you don't

want a bridal shower, engagement party, or bachelorette party?"

Meghan nodded. "I'm sure those would be fun times, but I have so much going on with the bakery, the barn, and wedding planning, and it would be too stressful to plan everything."

Jackie's eyes brightened. "I have an idea," she told her. "What if I plan your bachelorette party? I am such a good event planner, and I know how to make any gathering a good time. I'll give you the best bachelorette party you could imagine!"

"I don't know," she said nervously. "I'm not thrilled with the idea of going away again, especially since I just got back from Texas. I don't have the time or energy right now."

"Meghan, you will only get married *once*," Jackie countered. "This is a time in your life you will never get to do again! What if you give up on having a bachelorette party and regret it later? Is that what you want? Regrets?"

Her stomach dropped; she sensed she would not regret skipping out on a bachelorette party, but what if she was wrong? What if she looked back in five years and wished she had celebrated properly? Was Jackie *right*?

"You want to go! I can see it on your face."

Meghan bit her lip. "Between us, Jack and I were thinking about getting married earlier," she whispered. "Jack wants us to elope sooner rather than later; he thinks it would be romantic and help take the pressure off of our wedding in Texas. If we do that, I

don't think I can spare the time or money for a bachelorette party, Jackie."

Jackie winked at her. "Enough said. I can tell that you want to have a party, and it's official. I am taking control and planning your bachelorette party, and that is that! Don't you worry 'bout a thing. Leave everything to me, almost-Mrs. Irvin. I will make this a bachelorette party you will *never* forget!"

3

Three weeks later, Meghan found herself waiting in the security line at the Sandy Bay Airport. It was a damp, rainy morning, and she was in a terrible mood as she glanced at her watch. It was five-thirty, and Meghan was not a morning person; she wondered why Jackie had chosen an early flight to kick off her bachelorette party, and she hoped this was not a sign of how the rest of the weekend would go.

As she glanced out of the floor-to-ceiling windows along the corridor, she saw flashes of lightning that made her feel nauseated; what if her plane got caught in a storm? Meghan usually didn't worry about flying, but with the storm raging outside, she felt the knot in her stomach grow.

"I got the coffee you wanted," Jackie greeted her as she rejoined Meghan in line.

Meghan thanked her and took a sip of the drink, but she immediately knew Jackie had made a mistake. “Jackie! Does this have dairy in it?”

Jackie nodded. “It’s your usual drink, Meghan. A full-fat mocha latte.”

Meghan spat out the drink, not caring who saw her. “Jackie, I *told* you. I am lactose intolerant. The doctor confirmed it when I was home in Texas. We talked about this, and I reminded you before you went off to grab the coffee.”

Jackie huffed. “It’s not my fault your diet is complicated!”

“It i*sn’t* a diet,” Meghan growled. “It's intolerance. That is *completely* different.”

“Well sorry,” Jackie replied with an attitude. “Sorry, it wasn’t good enough for you.”

Meghan crossed her arms in front of her chest. Irritated didn’t even begin to describe how she felt; she wanted nothing more than to be home in her own bed, not in the airport at five-thirty in the morning for a bachelorette party she didn’t even want.

“Who else is coming?” she asked Jackie. “And where exactly are we going? I didn’t realize we were going this far out of town.”

Jackie raised an eyebrow. “That information is a *surprise*,” she scolded her. “You will just have to wait to find out.”

"MEGHAN!"

Meghan squinted through her sleepy eyes and saw her friend Karen from across the room. Karen was one of her dearest friends in Sandy Bay; they were close to fifty years apart in age, but Karen was the most athletic and spirited person Meghan knew.

"It's time for your little getaway!" Karen shrieked as she approached them. She was wearing a matching lavender tracksuit and her white-blonde bob bounced on her shoulders. "Are you excited, Bride-to-Be?"

Meghan hugged her friend, thankful Karen had been included. Karen was pragmatic and reasonable, and Meghan was happy to have someone with a good head on their shoulders invited to her bachelorette weekend.

"I'm sleepy, and Jackie is getting on my nerves," she whispered to Karen as they embraced. "Where are we going?"

Jackie marched over and tapped Meghan on the shoulder. "I heard that! Don't ask the girls where we are going; this is a surprise, Meghan!"

"Hi ladies."

The three women turned to see Trudy walking toward them. She was wearing a flamingo-print beach shirt with pink pants and a pink visor. "I'm ready for our trip."

Meghan smiled. "I'm glad you are here," she greeted.

"You look like you are ready for the beach. Are we

going to the beach, Jackie?"

Before Jackie could reply, Meghan spotted a familiar face in the crowd. It was Myrtle, her younger sister! Myrtle was twenty-one, but despite their age difference, she was Meghan's favorite sister. Myrtle was funny and kind, and she and Meghan looked like twins.

"What are you doing here?" she exclaimed.

"Jackie invited me," Myrtle grinned. "We have a three-day weekend at school, so I zipped up here to fly with you to your party."

Meghan felt tears brimming in her eyes. She turned to Jackie. "Thank you," she said sweetly, forgetting how frustrated she had been earlier. "Having my sister here means so much to me. Thank you for getting her here."

Jackie beamed. "I want you to have the best time, and I knew you would want Myrtle to be here!"

Meghan kissed her sister on the cheek. "This is perfect," she admitted. "All of my girls."

"Well, not all of them," Jackie told her. "There is one more guest coming."

"Who are we missing? Is Mama joining us? Or my other sisters?"

“Yoo-hoo!”

All the women looked over to see Sally Sheridan sashaying toward them. She was dressed in a red velvet mini-dress and matching heels. “It’s me, girls!” she called out. “I’m ready to party!”

Meghan stared at Jackie. “Why did you invite Mrs. Sheridan?” she hissed. “She’s already causing a scene and we haven’t even arrived at the party.”

Jackie glowered at her. “Don’t be rude,” she scolded Meghan. “She is your friend.”

Meghan pasted a smile on her face as Mrs. Sheridan walked up to them. “So good to see you,” she said as she kissed her cheek. “I am so happy you are coming.”

“This old gal is ready for a grand time,” Mrs. Sheridan gushed as she pulled a newly bedazzled cane out of her purse. “I even have the accessories for this party; look at my new cane!”

Jackie’s lips turned up in a huge smile. “That cane is ready to hit the scene in our destination.”

“Should we tell her where we are going?” Trudy asked mischievously.

“I think we should wait until we get there,” Karen teased.

Meghan glared at them. “Come on, ladies,” she urged. “Just tell me where we are going. I can’t stand the surprise any longer."

Jackie nodded. "Let's all say it on three," she ordered. "One... two... three…."

"WE'RE GOING TO LAS VEGAS!" the women cried.

Meghan's face paled. "Las Vegas?"

"Aren't you excited?" Karen asked. "I love Las Vegas! The weather is superb, and there are gorgeous mountains to go running in."

Trudy agreed. "And the bars and casinos aren't bad either!"

Meghan fought back tears. She had never had a desire to go to Las Vegas; she had never been a big partier, and the thought of trooping across the country to sit in loud bars and casinos sounded like torture to her. She had envisioned a relaxing weekend by a pool or ocean for her bachelorette party, and now, that dream was dead.

"I can tell she isn't happy," Jackie pouted as Meghan took a long breath. "I did all of this work to plan a perfect weekend for her, and she's upset."

Myrtle shook her head. "She's fine," she told Jackie brusquely. "She just isn't a morning person. Give her some time to wake up and she'll be good as new."

The group shuffled closer to the security line, and before Meghan knew it, she was on an airplane bound for Las Vegas.

A few hours later, she found herself shuffled into a van. "It's the complimentary shuttle to the hotel," Jackie explained as the woman climbed into the brown van. "It will take us there for free!"

Trudy beamed as she retrieved a pair of fake designer sunglasses from her patent leather purse and leaned back against her seat. "This is the life," she breathed. "Being chauffeured from the airport in a private van? Jackie, this is great!"

They drove for five minutes until they reached a street corner. Meghan squinted as the sun crept into her face. "Why are we stopping?"

Jackie shrugged. "For gas? I don't know."

The driver exited the van and threw open the sliding door. A crowd of middle-aged women crowded inside. "What are you doing?" Jackie cried. "This is our *private* shuttle to the hotel!"

The driver raised an eyebrow. "This isn't a private shuttle," he corrected her. "This is a public van. You paid online for the reservation, remember?"

Jackie's face turned beet red. "I don't know what you're talking about," she protested, but it was clear to the group that she was lying.

The driver helped the last middle-aged woman in and slammed the door shut.

"What are you in town for?" Karen kindly asked one of the women.

"My divorce was finalized last month," a curvaceous raven-haired woman explained. "My girls and I are out on the town to celebrate!"

"How lovely," Meghan grumbled. "We're in the company of middle-aged divorcees to celebrate my last few weeks as a single lady," she thought to herself.

"What are you in town for?" the newly divorced woman asked. "A conference? Gambling?"

"It's her bachelorette party," Myrtle explained as she pointed to Meghan. "My sister is getting married soon and we are here to celebrate her!"

One of the middle-aged women scoffed. "Ugh, girl, take my advice: don't do it. Marriage is so overrated."

"Yeah," another chimed in. "Marriage is for fools. Getting married the first time was the worst mistake of my life."

"What about your second time?" one of the others teased.

"That time was good," she winked.

Meghan crossed her arms over her chest. She was tired, cranky, and ready for a nap after a long morning with Jackie and the girls.

Thirty minutes later, they arrived at a shabby motel. "This must be where the ladies are staying," Myrtle whispered to her. "It looks gross. You'd think they would have chosen a better place to stay for her

divorce party."

The driver opened the door and beckoned to Meghan. "Alright, Bride-to-Be, here is your castle for the next three nights."

Meghan's jaw dropped. "This is where we're staying?" she hissed at Jackie as she surveyed the dilapidated motel. It was a two-story stucco structure with a drained swimming pool out front. A group of motorcyclists clad in leather pants and jackets sat by the empty pool, each with a cigarette in their hands. "This looks scary, Jackie. What is this?"

Jackie frowned. "It was a great price," she explained. "And it's walking distance to The Strip. The reviews online were fine, and I had a coupon I won at an auction a few years ago…"

Karen bit her lip, but ever the optimist, she smiled. "It *is* close to everything," she reassured Meghan as she glanced around. "And there is a lot of natural light by the pool!"

"The pool doesn't have any water in it," Meghan grumbled.

"Maybe we can fix that!" Myrtle added. "Why don't we go check-in? Jackie, lead the way."

Jackie guided the women inside to the main office. It was shabby and dark, with peeling green wallpaper and musty carpet. "Can I help you?" asked the receptionist as they trudged over to his desk.

"We're checking in," Jackie informed him. "This is the Truman Bachelorette Party."

"Oh, yes," he greeted them warmly. "I'm your receptionist, Todd Sherman. I'll be handling any issues or questions you may have during your stay."

"He seems nice," Myrtle whispered to Meghan.

"At least something about this dump is good," Meghan agreed.

Todd answered their questions and got them checked in. "And if you need anything, don't hesitate to let me know."

Jackie smiled at him and nodded, batting her eyelashes flirtatiously. "Thank you for your help."

She turned to the ladies and smiled at them. "I know this isn't the Plaza Hotel," she began. "But it will be perfect for our trip; the receptionist, Todd, is so nice... and cute... and he'll help us with anything we need."

"I can tell she's going to try to sneak a date in with him," Karen whispered to Meghan.

"I have something for all of you," Jackie continued as she zipped open her hot pink suitcase to reveal small pink party bags. "These are welcome gifts. Open them!"

She passed out a bag to each woman, a huge grin on her face. "Open them on the count of three. One... two... three!"

Everyone tore open their bag and pulled out a hot pink t-shirt. "They're matching party shirts!" Jackie cried in excitement. "One for each of us, and then a special one for Meghan! Put them on! We'll wear them out so everyone knows we're a bachelorette party!"

The ladies' shirts were hot pink and said BRIDESBABES in loopy cursive writing. Meghan saw Myrtle cringe, but she obediently put the shirt on over her maroon overalls.

"Meghan, look at yours!" Jackie commanded, and Meghan unfolded the white t-shirt. The font matched the other ladies', but it said ATTENTION! YOU'RE IN THE PRESENCE OF A PRINCESS BRIDE on the front. On the back were two angel wings painted on, and the bottom of the shirt had a frilly white tulle tutu attached.

She felt her cheeks burn as everyone stared at her; the shirt was horrendous, but she knew she would have to put it on. "It's nice," she choked as she slipped it on. "Thanks, Jackie."

"Anything for you!" Jackie sang as she pulled Meghan into a hug.

Meghan stiffened in Jackie's hug, but then, she

noticed Mrs. Sheridan was pointing out the front window of the lobby.

"Mrs. Sheridan?" she asked as she broke away from Jackie. "What's wrong?"

"Look, everyone," Mrs. Sheridan screeched. "He's alive! He's alive!"

Meghan looked at Myrtle and Karen in concern. "What is she talking about?"

Mrs. Sheridan's jaw dropped. "The King," she whispered as though she were in a trance. "The King! He's alive. He's *alive!*"

4

In walked a man dressed in an Elvis Presley costume. He wore a white jumpsuit, aviator sunglasses, and his jet-black hair styled just as Elvis' had been in his prime. Mrs. Sheridan screamed as she hobbled over to him and jumped into his arms. "I knew you were alive! I knew it!"

The Elvis impersonator grinned as he lowered Mrs. Sheridan to the ground. "The King could never die," he assured her as he winked at the group. "Music never dies, and neither do I!"

Mrs. Sheridan clapped her hands excitedly like a schoolgirl. "Would you sing for us?" she begged. "Sing Hound Dog! That's my favorite."

He smoothed his black hair away from his face and flashed a toothy smile at Mrs. Sheridan. "Anything for you, baby doll."

He broke into song, and Mrs. Sheridan closed her eyes and swayed along. Meghan had never seen her like this, and she chuckled as Mrs. Sheridan sang. When he finished his song, he batted his eyes at Myrtle. "What are you pretty girls here in Vegas for, anyway?"

Jackie pushed her way to the front of the group. "A bachelorette party!" she squealed. "Our friend is getting married... but I'm single!!"

He bit his lip and raised his eyebrows. "I'm happy to hear that you're single," he told her as Mrs. Sheridan fanned herself in excitement. "Who is the lucky lady who is getting married?"

Meghan raised her hand half-heartedly. "Me," she said. "I'm getting married."

The Elvis impersonator turned to her and shook her hand. "Congratulations," he wished her. "I wasn't the best at marriage… just ask Priscilla, my former wife… but from the looks of you, I'm sure you'll do just fine."

Jackie tapped his shoulder. "Mr. Presley, do you give private shows? I'd love to set something up... for my friend's party... could we exchange numbers?"

"It's only been five minutes and she's trying to get someone's number," Myrtle giggled quietly to Meghan.

He shook his head. "I don't do private shows, but I do have a standing set at The Venetian. I play every afternoon from two to three. You ladies should drop by."

"We would love that!" Jackie exclaimed.

"We'll be there today!" Mrs. Sheridan shouted joyously.

He winked. "Let me have my assistant give you tickets. Earl? Earl, come over here now!"

Meghan was shocked by how rudely he had spoken to his assistant, but she said nothing.

A stout man with thick wire glasses came over to them and produced an envelope from his vest. "I carry extra tickets around in case I meet pretty fans like you," he told the group as Earl gave him the envelope. "Here are tickets for the show this afternoon. I think you'll enjoy it."

Jackie nodded. "And in case we have issues? Can I get your business card?"

The impersonator licked his lips. "Of course," he told her as he pulled a silver card from his jumpsuit. "For you."

"Jeremiah Wilson," Jackie whispered. "I'm Jackie. It's nice to meet you."

Jeremiah bowed to Jackie, waved to the ladies, and then turned on his heel to leave. "Earl, let's go. We're running late because of you. Hurry up."

Meghan was again taken aback by Jeremiah's tone,

but she brushed it off, eager to get up to her room and rest a bit before they began their first day in Las Vegas.

After resting and relaxing in their rooms, it was time to go to the show. The ladies walked down the street to The Venetian, the luxury hotel that housed Jeremiah's show.

"I could have been happy staying here," Myrtle commented to Meghan as they walked into the ornate lobby.

It was like they had been transported to the finest hotel in Venice; there were paintings on the ceiling, marble pillars in every corner, expensive-looking furniture, and all the trappings of a luxury hotel.

"I wouldn't have minded splurging to stay here," Meghan agreed.

They followed small gold-plated signs to the theater and took their seats. Meghan reached into her purse and pulled out a small Tupperware container. Pamela had packed some snacks for the trip, and she happily dove into a serving of rhubarb pie.

"I want some," Myrtle told her, but Meghan brushed her off.

"I'm the PRINCESS BRIDE, remember?" she teased her sister. "The pie is ALL mine."

At exactly two in the afternoon, Jeremiah took the stage.

"He's gorgeous," Mrs. Sheridan announced loudly as other members of the audience laughed. "That Priscilla let a good one get away from her!"

Jeremiah, dressed in a blue jumpsuit and matching sunglasses, held a red electric guitar. "I'm gonna need a pretty lady to come up here and sing with me," he declared as the crowd whooped. Mrs. Sheridan waved her arms frantically, and Jackie stood up and waved. "I know there's a bachelorette party in the house tonight. Let's get the bachelorette herself to come up here and sing!"

Meghan's body grew hot, and she felt the blood rush to her head. She had no desire to go on stage, but her friends and sister were cheering her on. She rose from her seat and walked to the little metal stairs at the front of the stage, still holding her Tupperware dish of pie. Mrs. Sheridan followed along behind her. "I'm coming, and no one can stop me!"

The two women arrived on stage, and Jeremiah sloppily wrapped an arm around Meghan's shoulders. "Thanks for coming, ladies."

Meghan brushed him off, and Mrs. Sheridan took her place. "Thanks for having us," she batted her eyelashes.

The crowd cheered, and Meghan stared at Jeremiah's face. It was red and sweaty, and she heard him slur his speech as he waved the microphone in Mrs.

Sheridan's face. "Is he drunk?" she thought to herself.

He came back to Meghan, and he placed an arm

around her waist to pull her closer. "Baby girl, can I have a bite of that pie?"

She shrugged him off, and he reached a finger into her container, taking a bite of her pie. "Yum, delicious, just like you," he trailed off.

He began to sing, and Mrs. Sheridan clapped her hands. Meghan noticed how awkward his movements were; he looked like a broken puppet. In the middle of the song, his voice broke, and he collapsed on the stage.

Mrs. Sheridan screamed. "What's going on? Is this part of the show?"

Meghan bent down to check his pulse as the crowd began to panic. "We need some help here!"

Earl, the assistant, dashed onto the stage. He threw himself on top of Jeremiah, and his face paled. "He's dead," Earl declared with a haunted look on his face. "The King is dead. Elvis is *dead*!"

5

"This is the worst trip ever," Trudy complained as the women walked back to the hotel. "First, the hotel is trash, and now, Elvis *died* in the middle of the show? What's next, Jackie? Are they gonna haul one of us off to jail or something?"

Meghan had been thinking the same thing, but she was happy that someone else verbalized it. She didn't want to sound ungrateful; she knew Jackie had spent time and money organizing the trip, but a getaway to Las Vegas was truly the last thing she had wanted, and now, they were in the midst of a tragedy!

It was late afternoon now, and the sun was beating down on the women. "This t-shirt doesn't fit right," Mrs. Sheridan complained as she pawed at herself. "Jackie, you didn't get the size I asked for. I wanted a medium, not an extra small."

"That must be mine," Myrtle commented as she tugged at the end of her shirt. "I wanted the extra small."

Jackie's shoulders slumped. "I just can't do anything right, can I?" she lamented as they turned a corner and spotted their shabby lodging. "I tried my best, guys. Organizing a bachelorette party isn't easy, and it's not like I had a lot of help."

Karen interjected. "That isn't quite the case," she said. "I offered to help and to pay for a trip to the beach; Meghan has always wanted to go to the Florida Keys, and I believe I mentioned that several times…"

Trudy nodded. "I told you Vegas wouldn't be the place for her," she told Jackie. "You wouldn't listen."

Myrtle wrapped an arm around Meghan's shoulder. "Don't listen to them," she whispered. "Their squabbling is stressful, and you don't need stress right now before your wedding. How about this: if the party hasn't improved by Sunday night, we'll do a sister trip and make that your real trip? What do you think?"

Meghan leaned into her sister. "You're the best. Have I ever told you that?"

"Just a time or two or three," Myrtle replied with a smile on her face.

They arrived at the hotel, and the group went inside the lobby. "I hope Todd is here," Jackie told them as she adjusted her hair. "He'll be so upset to hear about the trauma we went through today!"

Myrtle rolled her eyes. "That girl…"

Mrs. Sheridan began to cry. "This was the last place I saw him alive and well," she wailed as she placed a hand dramatically on her heart. "The King was here, and now, he's gone."

Jackie sashayed up to the desk and rang the bell. A thin-faced woman appeared. "Is Todd in?" Jackie asked.

"No," she answered shortly. "His shift is *over*."

"Okay," Jackie replied. "Will he be back tomorrow?"

"How should I know?" the woman answered, snapping her gum and giving Jackie attitude. "I'm not the boss of him."

"Got it," Meghan said briskly. "Let's go, ladies."

The women retired to their rooms. Meghan slammed the door behind her and locked it; she was happy to have time away from the group. She was exhausted from the day's events; from the early flight, to the encounter with Jeremiah, to his unexpected death on stage at the show. She was ready for her bachelorette party to be over.

Meghan peeled the comforter off of the twin bed; disappointed at how it looked and felt, and she threw the blanket into a corner. She pulled her cell phone out of her purse and called Jack.

"Hey, babe!" he greeted her. "How is the party? Where are you girls?"

"Jackie brought us to Vegas," she said in a low voice. "It's awful, my love. The motel is gross, everyone is in a bad mood, and she bought this ridiculous shirt for me to wear."

Jack laughed. "You aren't really the bachelorette party type," he commented as Meghan sighed. "Jackie should have known that."

"She planned a great party for *Jackie*," she told her fiancé. "But this isn't what I want."

"I have an idea," Jack said. "Why don't you stick it out today? If you wake up tomorrow and want to come home, I'll buy a one-way ticket for you. Does that help?"

Meghan smiled. Jack always wanted to save the day, and she appreciated his eagerness to help. "It does," she confirmed. "That makes it a lot better; you're telling me that if I make it through the next twelve hours or so, I can come home."

"That's right," he agreed. "It sounds like it can't get much worse, so do your best to stick it out. I'm sure by the time you wake up tomorrow, you'll be rested and feeling better, and you won't even want to come home!"

Jack was wrong. Things got much worse; after they

bid each other farewell and hung up the phone, Meghan was going to settle in for a nap when she heard a shrill scream. She grunted as she rose from the bed and peeked into the hallway to see what was the matter.

She was shocked to find Mrs. Sheridan flailing her arms. "Stay in your room, Meghan!" she ordered as she danced from left foot to right foot. "Don't come out here!"

Meghan ignored the order and stepped into the hallway. She was shocked to see a police officer shaking her head at her. "Ma'am, I'm going to need you to step back inside your room."

"What's going on?"

"Meghan! Call my lawyer. Call Frank!" Mrs. Sheridan cried as the officer placed handcuffs on her wrists.

"What is going on?" Meghan asked again.

"You need to step back inside," the officer advised. "Or we are going to arrest you as well."

"You're *arresting* her?" Meghan replied in shock. "For what? What did she do? We've only been here for a few hours."

The officer looked Meghan in the eye. "She knows what she did," she stated firmly. "And she's going to need a lawyer as *soon* as possible."

6

Jackie burst into the hall as Mrs. Sheridan was led away. "What's going on?" she cried.

"I have no idea," Meghan told her. "But they're taking her down to the station! We need to go get her out."

Karen opened her door. "What is the ruckus about?" she grumbled. "I am trying to practice mindfulness, but you are all being too loud."

"They took her away!" Jackie announced dramatically. "The police came and took Mrs. Sheridan off to jail!"

Meghan shook her head. "Not quite," she informed Karen. "They came and took her away, but they didn't say they are putting her in jail."

Karen frowned. "Why did the police come?"

Meghan shrugged. "We don't know, but I think we need to go to the station as soon as we can. We need to make sure she is okay."

"I'll go," Jackie offered. "Meghan, let's take a taxi down there."

"I'll hold down the fort here," Karen said. "You girls should go now."

Forty-five minutes later, the taxi pulled up outside of the police station. "That will be fifty-three dollars," the driver told them.

Meghan nodded and looked at Jackie. "Are you going to pay?"

Jackie's eyes widened. "I don't have my wallet," she whispered. "We left in such a rush that I forgot it."

"Of *course* you did," Meghan muttered as she pulled her credit card out of her wallet and paid the driver.

They walked inside the station and ventured to the front desk. "We're here to see Sally Sheridan," Jackie told the receptionist. "I'm Jackie, and this is Meghan Truman."

"One moment, please."

The receptionist picked up a silver phone and made a hushed call. "The officers would like to speak with you two as well."

"WHAT?" Meghan asked in alarm. "Are we in trouble?"

A tall African American officer approached them. "Meghan? Jackie? I'm Officer Brady. Come this way, please."

They obediently followed him to a small room with three folding chairs and a metal table.

"What's the problem, Officer Brady?" Meghan asked. "My fiancé is a detective... I know how this works. Are we being detained?"

He shook his head. "I can't answer any questions, but I need to ask you a few things," he explained. "What are you doing in Las Vegas?"

"It's her bachelorette party!" Jackie declared, pointing her finger at Meghan. "She's getting married, and we are here with a group of women. We're innocently celebrating our friend."

Meghan cringed, wishing Jackie hadn't used the word "innocently", knowing it would only make the officer more suspicious.

"Is that true?" he asked Meghan.

She held up her left hand and flashed her engagement ring. "It's true, Officer Brady. This is my bachelorette weekend."

He pulled out his walkie-talkie and whispered something into it. A door opened, and Mrs. Sheridan walked in. "My friends," she cried as she hobbled over to them. "I am so happy to see you. You came to bust this girl out!"

"Settle down, Grandma," sneered the blonde officer who had escorted her in. "We need to corroborate your story. You aren't going anywhere yet."

"Grandma?" Mrs. Sheridan screeched. She raised her cane high in the air. "Say that one more time and I'll have your face meet my cane!"

Officer Brady held his hands up. "Ma'am, I am going to advise you to put the cane down," he ordered. "Or we will be charging you with assault."

She obeyed, but she glared at the blonde officer. "Now what?"

"You were seen harassing the deceased, Jeremiah Smith, by several eyewitnesses," the blonde officer told her. "You harassed him at the motel, and you followed Ms. Truman on stage at the show."

"He invited me!" Mrs. Sheridan shrieked. "I didn't follow her!"

Meghan raised an eyebrow but said nothing, and the officer saw the look on her face.

"Do you have something to add, Meghan?" the blonde officer asked.

"No," she stated. "I don't."

"She does!" Mrs. Sheridan insisted. "Meghan, Jackie, tell them that I am a nice lady and I would never

murder anyone! Tell them!"

"I told you to calm down, Grandma," the officer laughed.

Mrs. Sheridan's face darkened. "Don't say I didn't warn you," she glowered as she raised her cane.

Meghan dove to stop her, and Jackie began to scream. They tumbled into a pile, taking the officer down with them. Meghan felt Mrs. Sheridan fall on top of her, and she grimaced as her back cracked. "Owww," she complained. "Mrs. Sheridan, calm down. We need to get off of the floor."

The blonde officer rose to his feet, a stern look on his face. "You two took me down," he accused Meghan and Jackie.

"What?" Jackie asked. "We were trying to stop her. She was going to hit you with her cane, but we didn't let her."

"That's not how I saw it," Officer Brady commented. "I think the two younger ladies need to be placed in jail. They've caused enough trouble today. Send that Grandma back to my office and these two troublemakers to jail."

"To jail?" Meghan exclaimed. "I want my lawyer. You have to read me my rights and let me call my lawyer."

The officer laughed. "Maybe later. For now, you two are coming with *me*."

Before she knew it, Meghan had been put in handcuffs and led across the street to the Clark County Jail. She and Jackie were placed in a cell together, and Meghan collapsed in a corner, holding her legs and crying. She was exhausted, humiliated, and furious; she hadn't wanted to come to Vegas in the first place, and now, she was sitting on the floor of the jail.

"I can't believe this happened," Jackie casually commented as she picked at her cuticles. "Vegas is so crazy; this will make such a great story later."

"Are you kidding me?" Meghan asked. "You're thinking about what a great story this will make? You have to be joking."

Jackie laughed. "I think they were just flirting with us, Meghan," she assured her. "We aren't in real trouble."

"WE'RE IN JAIL, JACKIE!" Meghan screamed. "How do you not know we're in trouble?"

Jackie scowled. "You are such a pessimist," she told her. "I really don't think that's a good look for you."

Meghan narrowed her eyes at Jackie before turning her back and leaning her head against the white cement wall. She couldn't believe she was here, and she didn't know if Jack would be more outraged or embarrassed by the indiscretion.

"Jackie?!!"

Meghan turned to see Jackie squealing as she wrapped her arms around a statuesque brunette. "Is it really you, Kendall?"

Meghan stood up. "Who is this, Jackie?"

"It's my cousin!" she cried in excitement. "Kendall and I grew up together. She moved to Vegas to be a dancer when I was in high school, and she won the lottery the next year! Can you believe it?"

Meghan raised an eyebrow. Kendall was thin and pretty, but she was dressed scandalously; she wore a red leather skirt, thigh high boots, and lipstick the color of blood. "If she won the lottery, what is she doing in here?"

Kendall glared at her. "That ain't any of your business, Toots."

Jackie shook her head at Meghan. "Don't be rude," she muttered.

Meghan watched as the cousins chatted. "It was so sad when we fell out of contact," Jackie lamented.

Kendall nodded. "Money can get in the way of happiness," she sighed as she squeezed her cousin's hand. "And I let mine go to my head a bit."

Jackie shrugged. "It's fate that we met up here. Let's let the past stay in the past. I'm so happy to see you!"

Kendall winked at her. “I am so happy to see you! What are you doing here, Jackie? I thought you were married and a nice little wifey.”

Jackie’s face darkened. “Divorced,” she corrected. “Divorced and thriving; I own two businesses, and I am building my empire.”

Meghan cringed. She didn’t exactly consider Jackie’s salon and the barn to be part of any empire, but she said nothing.

“Why are you in the slammer?” Kendall asked. “This doesn’t seem like your type of place.”

“It’s a mistake,” Jackie assured her. “And you?”

“A mistake,” Kendall said slowly, but Meghan could tell she was lying. “I ran out of money a few years back. I’ve been in here before for some *other* things, but this time, it was a mistake.”

“I’m so sorry,” Jackie said. “Do you need anything? Can I help?”

Kendall’s eyes sparkled. “Since you asked….do you have any cash on you?”

Meghan could no longer bear to listen to their conversation. She turned back to the corner and huddled into a tiny ball, weeping as she fell into a fitful sleep.

7

After a long night in jail, Officer Brady showed up to release Meghan and Jackie. Jackie bid farewell to her cousin, and then Officer Brady escorted them into a holding room.

"Just some reminders," he began as they rubbed their sleepy eyes. "You are not permitted to leave Las Vegas; there are questions about Jeremiah's death that need to be answered, and we are not letting any suspects leave until we have answers."

"We are considered suspects?" Meghan shrieked. "Why? We were just here to pick up Mrs. Sheridan. How did that turn us into suspects?"

He shrugged. "That's not my information to share," he told them. "Mrs. Sheridan has been released to your friends, and she is also not allowed to leave."

Meghan nodded, hoping that Jackie would keep calm so they would be released. “Got it. Can we go now?”

He nodded. “Yes. Here are your things.”

He handed them their purses and walked them to the door. “Have a nice day, ladies.”

They stepped out into the dry, hot air and blinked, their eyes unaccustomed to the bright Nevada sunshine. “Let’s get a cab,” Jackie suggested. “The hotel is a few miles away, and I am too tired to walk.”

Meghan glared at her. “You want me to pay for another cab for you?”

Jackie rolled her eyes. “I’ll pay you back. Just hail a cab.”

Meghan dug through her purse and retrieved her wallet. “My debit and credit cards are gone,” she gasped. “I had them when we went inside the station.”

Jackie crossed her arms over her chest. “Let’s go back inside and get them; the officers must have taken them!”

Meghan shook her head. “I’m not going back in there. We’ll just have to walk back.”

They walked in silence for over an hour. Finally, they arrived back at the shabby motel. They found their friends waiting for them, all with worried looks on their faces.

"Meghan!" Myrtle cried as she ran to her sister. "We were so worried about you! Mrs. Sheridan told us what happened; are you alright?"

Meghan bit her lip. She was overwhelmed by the lack of sleep and events of the previous day. "I'll be fine," she murmured as she hugged her sister. "I just need to rest."

Trudy glared at Jackie. "This is the worst party, Jackie," she complained. "The hotel wouldn't let us eat breakfast here; they said that since you made the reservation, you had to check us in for breakfast. We all had to munch on Karen's carrot sticks instead of eating a real meal."

Jackie glowered. "You should have found a cafe or something," she grumbled. "It's not my job to feed you."

"But it was your job to keep this party running smoothly," Karen countered. "This has been a disaster, and we need to turn things around for Meghan."

The group turned to look at her, and Meghan felt her face growing hot. "I need to shower," she muttered as she tucked a messy lock of hair behind her ears. "I'm going upstairs."

After a nap and shower, Meghan returned downstairs to find the group waiting for her. "I have great news!" Jackie exclaimed as she rushed at Meghan. "The hotel owner dropped by and heard our group talking, and he wants us to have dinner here at the hotel for free!"

Meghan perked up, happy to hear even the slightest bit of good news. "Really? That's great. Where's Mrs. Sheridan?"

"She's napping," Karen informed her. "I think she's a little embarrassed, too."

A man's voice boomed, and the ladies turned to see a tall, portly man in a checkered suit walking toward them. "Ladies, welcome! I'm Lucky Elway, the owner of the hotel. Your friends told me about all the troubles you've had, and I want to provide a nice meal for the bride-to-be! I'm sorry Las Vegas has been such trouble, but I think a nice dinner here will make it all better."

Meghan shook his hand. "It's a pleasure to meet you," she greeted. "Thank you for your kindness; it is so appreciated."

"My pleasure," he assured her. "I am just happy to help. I need to go to take care of some business, but you ladies enjoy!"

Trudy grinned. "We can't turn down a free dinner. Let's go!"

She led the way into the small restaurant next to the lobby. "It looks fine," Myrtle commented as she read the menu. "They have salads and soups, and the breadbasket sounds great."

"Order whatever you want," Jackie commanded. "He told us to make ourselves at home, and I think we will!"

The women ordered many plates of food; Trudy ordered a pasta dish, Meghan asked for shrimp tacos, Karen ordered a salad, and the other women split a pizza. They were all happy to have stumbled upon some good luck *at last*, and the women were all smiles when the food appeared.

“This looks delicious,” Myrtle cooed as the waiter set the pizza in front of her.

“I’m so hungry!” Jackie told them as she picked up her fork.

Karen gave her a gentle slap on the elbow. “Stop, Jackie. Let Meghan eat first!”

Meghan winked at Karen as she placed the paper napkin in her lap and settled in. She picked up the first of three shrimp tacos, her mouth-watering as she smelled the fresh *pico de gallo*. She opened her mouth, took a bite, but before she could swallow, she spat it out.

“What’s wrong?” Trudy asked in alarm. “Are you okay?”

“It must be spoiled,” Meghan moaned as her stomach lurched. “The shrimp tastes rotten!”

Jackie took a bite of her pizza and had the same reaction. “This pizza is disgusting. Something must be wrong in the kitchen!”

All the ladies took bites of their meals, and each one had the same experience. “It’s terrible,” Karen lamented. “How can someone ruin a salad? That just seems impossible.”

Myrtle frowned. “I think we should leave and go somewhere else; no one is going to eat this, right ladies?”

Meghan nodded. “And to think... it seemed like things were on the up and up…”

“Hey,” Karen whispered as she pointed to a table in the corner. “At least we’re not as miserable as that guy.”

Meghan looked over and gasped. Sitting alone at the table, weeping into his bowl of spaghetti, was Earl Wilson, Jeremiah’s assistant.

8

Meghan rose from her seat and walked over to Earl, taking the seat next to him. “Are you alright?” she asked.

He retrieved a handkerchief from his pocket and blew into it. “I just don’t know what I’m going to do now.”

Meghan patted his back. She could see Earl was young, and he had the twang of a southern accent. “I’m so sorry your boss passed away.”

Earl stared at her. “He wasn’t just my boss,” he revealed. “He was my uncle.”

Meghan’s heart sank. Despite feeling frustration from her disastrous bachelorette party, she felt sorry for Earl; he looked so lost and alone, and she wanted to help him. “I’m so sorry for your loss,” she told him.

He shrugged. “You’re the only one who has said that

to me," he admitted. "Most people didn't like my uncle."

"Why?"

Earl buried his face in his hands, and Meghan could see his stout body shaking. "He could be a big jerk," he explained. "And he let Las Vegas take his morals and throw them out the window. He was a womanizer, and a cheat, and a cad, and he wasn't well-liked by our family."

Meghan raised an eyebrow. "Then how did you end up working for him?"

"I grew up on a farm in Alabama," he said. "My choices were to work on the family farm or make it on my own. One day, just after high school graduation, Uncle Jeremiah called my daddy up and told him he needed an assistant. I asked if I could do it, and that's how I ended up out here."

Meghan nodded. "It seems like everyone ends up out here in a different way," she offered. "Did you like working with him?"

Earl wiped a tear from his ruddy cheek. "Not really," he whispered. "He was a jerk to me, but the money was good, and I have so many brothers and sisters back home in Alabama... I needed the money, and I dealt with whatever he threw at me."

"What are you going to do now?" Meghan asked gently. "Do you know anyone who can help get you another job? Surely he had some contacts in this town?"

Earl blew his nose. "Everyone hated him," he lamented. "No one will want to work with me. I don't know what I'm going to do. I have no real skills or college education. All I know how to do is assist performers. I'm doomed! I'm going to have to go back to the south."

Earl was melting down, and Meghan knew everyone in the dingy restaurant was staring at him. She patted him on the shoulder. "I'm so sorry," she repeated. "I'm sure you'll be able to find another job. Maybe check here at the hotel?"

He wiped his nose and nodded. "I might do that. Thanks for your help…?"

"Meghan," she introduced. "I'm Meghan Truman."

Once Earl had collected himself, Meghan returned to her table. "What was that about?" Myrtle whispered. "Wasn't that guy the Elvis impersonator's assistant?"

"He was," Meghan confirmed. "And he is his nephew. Can you believe that?"

Jackie tossed her hair and quickly pinched her cheeks. "What is she doing?" Myrtle asked.

"A man must be approaching," Meghan muttered. She was right. Todd Sherman, the receptionist, came up to their table.

"Ladies," he greeted. "How are we this evening?"

"Not great," Trudy answered truthfully. "This dinner is horrible."

Todd frowned. "I am so sorry to hear that, ladies," he apologized. "Would you allow me to make a reservation for you down the street at a different restaurant? I know the executive chef at Kabuto, Las Vegas' most acclaimed sushi restaurant and could you get you a deal, and then perhaps we could go out on the town?"

"No way," Meghan muttered under her breath. "We've let this trip get out of control, and we aren't going to trust a stranger. That just seems like bad judgement."

Trudy placed her hands on her hips. "Meghan," she murmured. "Get a grip! Todd wants to take us out, and we should let him."

"What was that, ladies?"

"Nothing!" they cried in unison.

"I think we should go," Jackie declared. "Let's live a little."

Meghan rolled her eyes. "We've been to jail, seen a dead man, and nearly gotten food poisoning, and you want to do more?"

Karen frowned at Meghan. "I think you need to adjust your attitude," she hissed. "You've been in a sour mood this whole time. I know it hasn't been the weekend of your dreams, but Meghan, you need to let go of your expectations and have a good time. You're the one holding yourself back here."

Meghan's jaw dropped. "Karen!"

Karen shook her head. "You need to rethink your attitude, sister. If you don't, you are going to ruin this trip for everyone. It hasn't been all bad, and you know it. Just be grateful we all get to spend this time together."

Meghan stared at Karen as she walked off. She was stunned by Karen's words, and she weighed them carefully. Was she ruining the trip for everyone? Did she need an attitude adjustment?

"Ladies?" Todd asked. "What do you say? Let your favorite hotel receptionist and part-time Vegas tour guide take you to dinner!"

Meghan took a deep breath. "We'll do it," she said shakily. "Let's go."

Four hours, one magnificent sushi dinner, two bars, four clubs, and a visit to Encore Beach Club later, the women arrived back at the motel. Their makeup was smeared, their hairdos were flat, their feet were sore, but they were filled with excitement after the best night out they had ever had.

"That was a blast," Myrtle commented as she sank into a dingy green armchair in the hotel lobby. Her wavy hair was knotted and dirty, but she had a grin on her face.

"I'm glad you girls had fun," Todd told them as he waved goodbye. "Get some rest, and maybe we can do it all again tomorrow!"

The women shuffled upstairs to their rooms. When

Meghan closed her door, she smiled in spite of herself. Karen had been right; it had been a fun night out, and she was grateful she had let her bad attitude go.

She threw herself onto the stiff bed, but before she could crawl beneath the covers, the room phone rang. "Hello?"

"Miss Truman?"

"Yes?"

"This is Belinda, the night time receptionist. You have someone waiting for you down here in the lobby. They would like you to come right down."

She glanced at her watch. It was three in the morning. Who could possibly be waiting for her?" She rose from the bed, hurriedly tying back her hair. She was going to find out.

9

She anxiously walked downstairs, unsure of what was waiting for her at such a late hour in the night. Was Jack here to surprise her? Had he come to Vegas? She hoped it was him, and she felt her lips turned upward into a smile as she imagined running into his arms.

Instead, she saw that the lobby was empty except for a middle-aged woman. She was sitting alone in a shabby yellow armchair, her face drawn and her arms crossed over her chest.

Meghan approached the woman. “Hi there. I’m Meghan. They called and said you wanted to see me?”

The woman glared at Meghan, her green eyes bright with rage. She tucked her chin-length black bob behind her ears and stood up. “You killed my husband.”

Meghan was taken aback. “What? Excuse me?”

The woman pointed a finger in Meghan’s face. “You heard me! You killed my husband, Jeremiah Wilson.”

“You’re his *wife*?”

She nodded. “Of twenty-seven years. I’m Louise Wilson, and I’m here to find out why you did what you did.”

Meghan felt her heart beating furiously in her chest. Louise looked angry, and Meghan didn’t want to cross an angry stranger. “I don’t know what you’re talking about…” she stammered. “I didn’t even know your husband.”

Louise smiled creepily. “Of course you did,” she insisted. “You were on stage with him when he died. You fed him the Rhubarb pie! I know in my gut that that’s how you poisoned him. What did he ever do to you? Did he look at you the wrong way? Did he flirt with you? Is that why you decided to kill him?”

Meghan’s jaw dropped. “This is ridiculous,” she muttered. She looked over to the reception desk where Belinda was reading a fashion magazine. “Belinda, can you have her removed? I’m going back to bed.”

Louise winked at her. “I paid Belinda good money so that she would turn a blind eye to this visit,” she informed her. “It’s just you and me down here, and you are going to tell me what happened to my husband and why you killed him.”

Louise pulled a dagger out of her purse and held it in

front of Meghan's nose. "Sit down," she ordered, and Meghan obeyed.

"What do you want?" Meghan asked nervously as she eyed the end of the dagger.

"I want to know why you killed him," Louise repeated. "What did he ever do to you?"

Meghan shook her head. "I didn't have anything to do with it," she insisted. "I was on stage, and then he collapsed."

"Because of your pie."

"No," Meghan corrected. "I ate the pie too! I don't know where you got that idea, but it's ridiculous. All of my friends ate it too."

Louise's eyes widened. "They did?"

"Yes," Meghan told her. "They did. My pie couldn't have killed him since we ALL ate it. Your theory is impossible."

"I see," she murmured backing away from Meghan. She collected herself and placed her hands on her hips. "I'm warning you, Meghan," she began again. "Stay out of my way, or else."

Louise turned on her heel and stormed out of the hotel. Meghan marched over to the desk. "Thanks a lot, Belinda," she said sarcastically as Belinda continued to eye her magazine. "You let a stranger off the street harass one of your guests, all because she paid you off? I hope you know that I'm leaving this hotel a terrible review when I leave."

Belinda said nothing and continued to snap her gum. Meghan stomped out of the lobby and into the night. She was livid, and she needed to take a walk to clear her head. The lights on the strip were bright as she made her way down the block, and she marveled at the replica of the Eiffel Tower, the beautiful ferris wheel, and the magnificent fountains lining both sides of the street. "It sure is different than Sandy Bay," she thought to herself as she walked down the block.

She looked at her watch. It was nearly five in the morning, and she knew Jack would be awake for work. She pulled out her phone and gave him a call. "Babe?"

"Hi, honey," he answered sweetly. "How is my lovely fiancé? You're up early!"

She told him what had happened with Louise, and he laughed. "You sure are getting into a lot of trouble out there," he remarked.

She was flabbergasted. "Did you not hear me?" she asked. "A stranger came into the hotel lobby and threatened me with a dagger, Jack! Aren't you worried about me?"

"I know you can always hold your own, babe," he assured her. "I don't worry about you. You're tough as nails."

Meghan was annoyed. She wanted Jack to share in her rage and fear, and he was dismissing her negative

experiences in Las Vegas as though they were minor.

"How was your night?" he asked.

"Besides being cornered by a stranger in the lobby, it was good," she informed him. "We had a great sushi dinner and went out."

"See?" he cried. "You had a good time! Just keep up the fun and everything will be okay. You'll be home soon, and we'll be laughing about this before you know it."

She felt her stomach churn, and she felt tears brim in her eyes. She would not be home soon, at least not until the police gave her permission to leave, and all she wanted to do was return to her normal life with her job, her dogs, and Jack.

"Just hang in there, babe," he told her. "Things will work out. They always do!"

She said goodbye to her fiancé, feeling annoyed. The sun was beginning to rise, and she decided to return to the hotel.

She walked with her head hung, staring at her feet as she trudged along The Strip. She had a dull ache in her head from exhaustion, and her eyes were swollen from crying. Meghan had never felt so miserable, and as she walked, she cursed herself for agreeing to come on a surprise trip thrown by Jackie. She should have known things would get out of control.

As she passed the large lighted fountains outside of Caesar's Palace, a famous hotel and casino, she noticed two animals running toward her. "Are there wild animals in Las Vegas?" she worried to herself as they approached.

She sighed in relief when she realized the two animals were friendly dogs, both wagging their tails and licking Meghan's hands.

"Hi, babies," she murmured as she knelt down to stroke their faces. The two dogs looked to be a mixed breed, but their fur was the same texture as Fiesta and Siesta, Meghan's beloved twin dogs. "What are you doing out here?"

She reached for their necks and read their collars. "There's no phone number here," she muttered. "But your names are on your collars. Sunny and Rainy. What adorable names!"

Sunny sniffed Meghan's legs and licked her on the cheek. Rainy tried to crawl into her lap. She laughed, happy to have found some friendly residents of Las Vegas at last. The trip had been difficult, but at the moment, finding friendly dogs made it all feel better.

"Sunny, Rainy, you are too cute," she laughed as Rainy wagged her tail back and forth. "Your collars don't have any contact information on them, and I don't want to take you to the shelter. I think you might have to come back to the hotel with me."

She wondered if they would follow her, and she stood from the ground. "Come on, girls!"

The dogs did not move. "Come on," she repeated. "I

can't leave you out here on the streets."

"SUNNY! RAINY!"

Meghan turned to find a bald man sprinting toward them. "Oh, my sweet girls!" he exclaimed as he dashed to the dogs. "Thank goodness you are alright."

The two dogs jumped up and down, excited to see their master. "I found them wandering around," Meghan explained. "I checked their collars, but they didn't have any contact information."

He shook his head. "My wife and I have been meaning to update their collars for months," he told her. "But we never got around to it. Clearly, we need to! I was taking them out for a walk before I went to my office, but when I bent over to tie my shoes, they got away from me. I'm glad they were safe with you."

She smiled at him. "I love dogs," she said. "I have two sweet little dogs at home. I've been missing them a lot, so running into your fur babies has been a treat."

Sunny turned to Meghan and licked her on the knee. "They've really taken to you," the man laughed. "You really have a way with dogs. What kind do you have?"

“I’m not sure,” she admitted. “I kind of inherited them from a friend. They’re precious, though, and I’m glad they are mine.”

The man nodded. “What brings you into town? Are you visiting the city?”

“Bachelorette party,” she explained, the smile on her face disappearing.

“Yikes,” he replied. “Not going well? Is the bride being difficult?”

“It’s the opposite,” she grumbled. “I am the bride. My friends are being difficult.”

“Wow! A bride-to-be. Congratulations.”

“Thank you,” Meghan responded, trying her best to be polite. “I’m excited to get married, but not so excited to be here.”

He nodded. “I get that. Las Vegas is not for the faint of heart. Where are you from?”

“The Pacific Northwest,” she answered. “A small town. It’s quaint and quirky, but I love it. The sea air is unbeatable, and the people are genuine.”

“That sounds incredible!”

“It is,” she replied. “And you? Are you a Vegas native?”

“My wife and I are both from the East Coast and are

really aching to get out of here. We're both doctors, so we're working on getting a transfer to a hospital in Florida… hopefully somewhere near the sea."

"That sounds amazing," she remarked. "Florida sounds much better than Vegas."

"It is," he agreed. "My wife actually did her

bachelorette weekend on Anna Maria Island, a small island off Florida's west coast. She had a low-key weekend with yoga, massages, and dolphin watching."

"That sounds perfect," Meghan sighed. "Maybe I'll have to have another bachelorette party someday… maybe after I've been married a while."

"I'm sure that would be nice," he told her. "The dogs and I need to get going, but it was nice to meet you!"

"You as well," she said as she waved goodbye. "If you and your wife ever find yourselves in Sandy Bay, you should stop by my bakery. It's called Truly Sweet. I own it and run it, and I could get you some yummy treats."

He grinned. "That would be truly sweet! See you later. Take care!"

Her spirits lifted; it was amazing how the kindness of a stranger could improve her mood, and Meghan smiled as she continued her walk back to the hotel. "Maybe this city isn't that bad after all," she thought as she rounded the corner and saw the hotel in the distance.

When she arrived, she noticed a commotion around the entrance, and her heart sank.

"What is going on?" she wondered as she approached the front door. "What could possibly be going wrong *now*?"

10

Meghan peered ahead to see what was going on, and she felt a lump in her throat as she observed a large news crew stationed in front of the hotel.

A petite blonde anchor was talking to the camera, and Meghan could hear her loud voice projecting over the crowd. “WE now know WHO killed Elvis and just how he died! Stay tuned to find out MORE!”

Meghan put a hand over her face, hoping she could escape the attention of the news crew, but the reporter spotted her and waved her over. “Hey! Are you staying in this hotel?”

The cameraman looked into Meghan’s eyes. “Aren’t you the girl who was on stage with him?”

“That’s her!” the anchor shrieked. “That’s Meghan

Truman. She was there when he died!"

The crowd rushed over to her, and Meghan could hardly breathe. "Miss Truman, how well did you know Elvis?"

Meghan awkwardly shifted as someone shoved a microphone in front of her. "Not well," she said. "He was here at the hotel once…"

"He was here with you? At the hotel? You had him over to your hotel room? Were you having an affair with him at the hotel?" the anchor pressed.

"No!" Meghan cried. "Of course not!"

The anchor raised an eyebrow. "You were having an affair with him somewhere other than the hotel? Is that what you are trying to say?"

"No!" she insisted. "I barely knew him."

"So, you were having an affair with a man you barely knew?"

She couldn't take it any longer. Meghan pushed past the crowd and barreled into the hotel to find her friends and sister sitting in the lobby. "What is going on?" she wailed. "Why is the press here?"

"How are you? And where were you?" Myrtle asked as she raced to her sister's side. "We were worried about you, Meghan!"

"You can't just take off in the middle of the night in

Las Vegas," Karen chastised her. "Anything could have happened to you."

Jackie placed her hands on her hips. She was dressed in an obnoxiously bright orange t-shirt. "There you are!" she exclaimed. "We were worried about you!"

Meghan raised an eyebrow as she studied Jackie's shirt. Her jaw dropped as she realized the image on the front was *her* face.

"What are you wearing?" she shrieked as she read the words clumsily printed above her picture on the shirt. The shirt read "I Know What Elvis' Killer Did Last Night".

"Jackie! What are you wearing? Where did you get that shirt?"

"I had it made," Jackie informed her. "I ran down to a printer earlier and had it done. What do you think?"

Meghan placed her hands on her face in exasperation. "It's terrible!" she yelled. "What were you thinking? You can't walk around like that?"

"Meghan, it's a great idea," she insisted. "My cousin brought it up to me while we were waiting in the jail cell. She thought it would be a good idea and an easy way to make money."

Meghan narrowed her eyes at Jackie. "You think wearing a shirt that slanders my name and reputation is a good idea?"

Jackie laughed. "I don't just want to wear it," she explained. "I want to sell these shirts! We could make so much money off of these babies right now while

the story is hot. Talk about an easy way to make some money. We won't even have to gamble!"

Myrtle placed her hands on her hips. "You need to march upstairs and take off that shirt *now*," she growled at Jackie.

"Or what?"

"Or you are going to be sleeping outside tonight," Karen finished. "I don't care if you want to make a quick buck, but you aren't going to ruin Meghan's reputation while you do it."

Jackie scowled. "You can't tell me what to do."

"Oh yes, I can," Meghan said. "It's *my* party. I am the bachelorette. You've done enough damage, Jackie, and you aren't going to add this to your list of disasters."

"Just do what she says," Trudy ordered as everyone glared at Jackie. "Go on."

Jackie turned on her heels and stomped away from the group.

"That girl," Karen muttered.

"She is something else," Trudy confirmed.

Myrtle stared at Meghan. "Now that we've finished that conversation," she said. "Talk to us, Meghan. Where did you go? Where have you been?"

Meghan shrugged. "I needed to clear my head," she

explained. "I needed some air. I just didn't expect to come back and find a news team at the hotel. What is going on?"

"You know what's going on," a shaky voice insisted. Meghan saw Mrs. Sheridan emerge from a corner. "You know what happened."

The group gasped. Mrs. Sheridan hadn't joined them for their night out, and they hadn't really seen her in almost a full day. She looked terrible; her face was gaunt, her hair was messy, and her eyes were red. "What's wrong, Mrs. Sheridan?" Karen asked. "Are you okay?"

Mrs. Sheridan pointed to Meghan. "She killed the King," she said in a sinister voice.

"What?" Meghan screeched. "What are you talking about?"

"You know what I am talking about!" Mrs. Sheridan insisted. "You killed the King! You killed him, and we all saw you do it."

Myrtle got in front of Meghan and stared into Mrs. Sheridan's face. "Take that back," she ordered. "Take back the nasty things you're saying about my sister."

Mrs. Sheridan shook her head. "No," she told Myrtle. "I can't. Everything I said is true, and I won't rest until justice is served. She killed Elvis, and we all know it!"

Meghan glared at Mrs. Sheridan. "I can't believe you would say something like that to me," she told her. "I thought you were my friend."

Mrs. Sheridan spat on the ground beside Meghan. "I'm not friends with *killers*," she glowered. "You killed the King, and I am going to get my revenge on you if it's the last thing I do!"

11

Mrs. Sheridan stormed away, and Meghan buried her face in her hands. "What was that all about?" Myrtle asked as Meghan cried.

"I have no idea!" she told her sister as Myrtle patted her back. "Mrs. Sheridan has lost her mind. You know I had nothing to do with that guy dying, right?"

"Of course, we know that," Karen assured her. "Mrs. Sheridan is off her rocker. Don't listen to a word she says."

"I just don't get why she believes I had something to do with Jeremiah dropping dead," Meghan lamented. "He seems like the typical Vegas type… you know, the kind of guy who drinks and smokes and parties all night long. Of course, he dropped dead on stage... he was probably long overdue to drop dead!"

Myrtle hushed her sister. "You might want to keep those comments to yourself," she hissed as she stroked Meghan's hair. "Why don't you go upstairs and get some sleep? You've been up most of the night, and I think some shut-eye could help you."

She nodded. "I think you're right," she said. "I'll go get some shut-eye."

Meghan's plan, however, was cut short; she had just changed into fresh pajamas and climbed into bed when she heard banging on her door.

"Who is it?"

"Management. Open up!"

She groaned as she rose from the bed and put on her slippers, padding to the door and hoping they didn't need anything important. "Can I help you?" she asked as she opened the door to find Belinda standing before her.

"You've brought shame to this hotel," Belinda stated firmly, a glare on her face. "There is a flock of reporters outside, and they are screaming obscenities at our guests!"

Meghan raised an eyebrow. "How is that my fault?" she asked. "How did I bring shame on your hotel? I didn't ask the press to camp out here."

Belinda tightened her hands into fists. "Were you on stage with Elvis when he died? That's what the reporters are saying, and if that's true, then you are the reason there is such a ruckus here!"

Meghan bit her lip. "I was on stage when he died," she began. "But he chose me to come on stage! I didn't want to go. And I wasn't the only one up there. Another one of my friends, Mrs. Sheridan, was there!"

Belinda gasped. "So there are more of you causing trouble here? That explains a lot! I've had a number of calls this morning about a wild bachelorette party causing trouble in Las Vegas, and it's YOUR party!"

Meghan shook her head. "This is ridiculous," she told her. "I want to file a complaint against this hotel. You are intruding on my privacy, insulting me, and I have had enough."

Belinda smirked. "No, I have. You have to leave *now*. It's my right to ask guests to leave, and I am asking you to go."

"No," Meghan told her. "I'm not going anywhere! This is my party, and we are staying."

Belinda glared at her. "Everyone knows you killed Elvis. Everyone knows about your dirty little affair. Why don't you and your trashy friends get out of here before more trouble hits?"

Meghan's eyes widened. "Affair? What affair? I'm engaged to be married! I'm not having an affair."

"I hope your fiancé sees this!" Belinda cried as she ran into Meghan's room and turned on the television.

The channel was set to a news station, and Meghan grimaced as she saw her face on the screen. It was the

footage taken only moments earlier in front of the hotel.

“Miss Truman, how well did you know Elvis?”

Meghan cringed as she stared at her face on the screen. “Not well,” she had said. “He was here at the hotel once…”

“He was here with you? At the hotel? You had him over to your hotel room? Were you having an affair with him at the hotel?”

“No!” Meghan cried. “Of course not!”

The anchor raised an eyebrow. “You were having an affair with him somewhere other than the hotel? Is that what you are trying to say?”

“No!” she insisted. “I barely knew him.”

“So you were having an affair with a man you barely knew?”

Belinda turned off the television. “It’s clear as day that you were having an affair with him! It went wrong, didn’t it? That’s why you killed him?”

“I didn’t kill anyone!” Meghan told her. “Get out of my room.”

Belinda shook her head. “Get your things and get out of my hotel, or I’ll call the police.”

Wanting to avoid another trip to the Clark County Jail, Meghan complied, quickly packing her things

and dashing down to the lobby.

"What is going on?" Trudy asked, the concern clear on her face. "A staff member just kicked me out of my room."

"Me too," Karen told them as she appeared with her paisley duffle bag. "They told me that our party was out of control and we have to leave."

Jackie flounced down the stairs with her three purple suitcases. "Can you believe this ill-treatment?" she cried. "Meghan, why did you have to get us in this trouble?"

"Me?" Meghan shrieked. "I didn't do anything wrong!"

Myrtle waved her hands to get their attention. "Guys! Something is wrong with Karen!"

The group looked over and saw Karen hobbled over. She was breathing heavily, and her face was pale. "What's wrong?" Trudy asked her. "Are you okay?"

Karen clutched her chest. "I think I'm having a panic attack," she said through gritted teeth. "Being kicked out of a hotel brought back some bad memories from my younger days, and I am not doing so well. I think I need a doctor."

Meghan ran to the front desk. "Belinda, call a doctor," she ordered as Belinda rolled her eyes at her.

"I'm not listening to you," Belinda told her. "You're a murderer and an ex-guest. Why would I help you?"

Meghan stared at her with dark eyes. "Call a doctor or I will march outside, get the attention of the press, and get them to come in here. I will tell them that someone is having a medical emergency and the manager of this hotel is refusing to call a doctor. If something happens to her, then you will be considered a murderer!"

Belinda sprang into action. "I'll have a doctor called over in a few minutes," she told Meghan. "And I'll let you stay here another night... under one condition."

"Yeah?"

"You'll help do dishes in the kitchen here."

"What?"

Belinda sighed. "One of our kitchen staff members called in sick tonight, and we are low on numbers. If you all help, I will help you."

"Fine," Meghan told her. "Whatever it takes to get a doctor for my friend."

Seven long minutes later, a doctor ran into the lobby. She knelt beside Karen, taking her blood pressure and pulse. "Are you having headaches?"

"No," Karen responded. "I think the worst of it is over."

The doctor took Karen's temperature and frowned. "The panic attack may be over, but you are running a high temperature," she noted. "I'm going to insist that you are taken to the hospital for a full examination."

Karen began to argue, but Meghan hushed her. "You are into your seventies," Meghan said softly. "Your health is the most important thing you have. Please let them take you in and check you out. For me? It can be my wedding gift!"

Karen gave her a soft smile. "Only for you," she told Meghan. "I'll go in."

A while later, the ladies waved goodbye as Karen was loaded into an ambulance and rushed off to the hospital. Upon hearing the rest of the ladies would have to tackle a mountain of dishes, Jackie climbed in the ambulance. "I'll make sure she's okay!" she called out as they closed the doors.

"That woman always manages to get out of doing the dirty work," Trudy muttered as they walked inside where Belinda was waiting for them with a box of aprons.

"Put these on and follow me."

They donned their aprons and walked back to the kitchen. "You'll be doing all of the lunch and dinner dishes from last night," Belinda informed them.

"Then, if there is a lull, you'll do yesterday's breakfast dishes."

Myrtle groaned, but Meghan elbowed her in the side. "Shhhh," she told her sister. "If we do this, we can stay another night, and the last thing we need right now is to be in Las Vegas without a place to stay."

"You're right," Myrtle agreed. "Let's get to washing

those dishes."

Meghan put on a pair of yellow rubber gloves and sighed. She hadn't thought her bachelorette party could get any worse, but here she was, covered in soap and grime and with a thousand dirty dishes in front of her.

12

As the ladies finished up the dishes and headed back to the lobby, Meghan could hardly keep her eyes open; she had been awake for far too long, and she was more than ready to get to bed. It was nearly nine in the evening, and while the other women were chatting about getting dressed and going out, she knew she needed to lay low.

"THE KING IS BACK!"

The women glanced at the staircase as Mrs. Sheridan hobbled down the stairs. "The King! Look, girls!"

They followed her gaze and saw she was pointing out the window at another Elvis impersonator. "That isn't the same guy…" Myrtle began, but Meghan shushed her.

"Let her believe it's the same guy, or she'll never let

the 'Jeremiah dying on stage' situation go," Meghan hissed. "Seriously, Myrtle, we have to play this up like it's the same person."

Myrtle nodded and went to the front door to wave in the Elvis impersonator. "Hey, come on in!" she greeted.

Meghan gasped as she stared at him. It was Earl. "What are you doing?" she asked quietly as Mrs. Sheridan rushed at him and began to fawn.

"I love you! The King is ALIVE! He's alive, everyone!" Mrs. Sheridan chirped. "It's so good to see you! I was so worried about you!"

Meghan caught Earl's gaze and mouthed, "FAKE IT" to him, and he began a full Elvis impression. He smiled and winked at Mrs. Sheridan. "I'm happy to see you too, baby doll."

Mrs. Sheridan planted a hand dramatically on her forehead. "All of this excitement has tuckered me out. I need to lie down."

She pretended to faint, and Earl ran to catch her as her body went limp. "Are you okay?" he cried as he fell out of character, his southern accent coming through.

"I think I need to rest on the couch," she whispered.

Meghan rolled her eyes. "Mrs. Sheridan," she said sharply. "Why don't you just go upstairs if this excitement is too much? Myrtle, can you please take her to her room."

Myrtle sprang into action, jumping up and escorting Mrs. Sheridan away. Meghan felt relieved; she was so irritated by Mrs. Sheridan's antics, and she could have a proper conversation with Earl if she weren't around.

"Meghan?" Trudy said softly. "Mrs. Sheridan left her cell phone down here. Look."

Meghan saw the phone. "I'll just give it to her later."

"Frank's calling," Trudy observed. "You should take it up now. You and I both know they need to hash out whatever has been going on between them."

"Fine," she grumbled. "I'll take it to her."

She walked upstairs, passing Myrtle on her way back down. "Don't ask," she cautioned as she moved past her.

She reached Mrs. Sheridan's room and knocked on the door. "Hello?"

Mrs. Sheridan answered the door. She was dressed in her pink bathrobe and a matching hairnet. "I was just settling myself down," she told Meghan. "Do you need something?"

She held up the phone. "Frank is calling."

Mrs. Sheridan rolled her eyes. "I don't want to talk to

him," she said.

Meghan spotted a framed picture next to Mrs. Sheridan's bed. "Oh, you should talk to him," she

said as she picked up the photo. "You love him so much that you brought a photo of hi—wait. This isn't you and Frank."

"It isn't," Mrs. Sheridan confirmed. "Look closely."

Meghan stared in shock. "That's you and the *real* Elvis Presley!" she exclaimed.

"That was taken here in Las Vegas," Mrs. Sheridan explained. "I came here on a trip after my first husband passed away. I was young and bitter, and I hoped the bright lights of Vegas would help heal my heart… or at least give me a reason to smile."

"Did it help?"

"The trip was terrible!" she declared. "The girls I came here with were snotty and they quarreled the whole time. One night, I decided to go out to a casino alone, and they were so angry with me."

"Did the trip get any better?" Meghan asked. Mrs. Sheridan's experience had a lot of parallels to her own, and she hoped the story improved.

"It did," she grinned. "When I was waiting for the bus to go to the casino, I got splashed by a car. It was raining hard, and I was soaking wet. I looked like a drowned mouse! As I started to cry, a limo pulled up beside me. The passenger rolled down his window, and I nearly died when I realized it was Elvis Presley!"

Meghan's eyes widened. "Are you serious?"

"Yes!" Mrs. Sheridan nodded. "He had seen me get splashed, and he felt bad. He invited me into his limo, and we spent the evening gallivanting around this city!"

"There's no way…" Meghan muttered in disbelief.

"It happened," Mrs. Sheridan insisted. "Look at the photo! He took me to the nicest restaurant in the city, and we shared a bottle of two-hundred-year-old Cabernet. That was his favorite bottle at the time. When we were through, he whisked me over to the theater where he was performing, and let me hang out in his dressing room while he warmed up. That's where we took the photo."

Meghan's jaw dropped. "Why didn't you tell me that?" she asked. "What an incredible story. I wish I had known that all along. It explains why you are so crazy for Las Vegas."

Mrs. Sheridan winked. "Some adventures are best kept to oneself. I just thought you could use some cheering up during this trip; remember, it may not be your ideal vacation, but something incredible could happen at any time."

Meghan hugged her. "Thank you for sharing that," she told her. "You've really cheered me up."

Mrs. Sheridan swatted her playfully on the bottom. "Now that you're cheered up, you should go rejoin the group," she ordered kindly. "Go have fun."

Meghan nodded and left the room, smiling to herself

as she walked back downstairs. "That woman…"

Earl greeted her when she returned. His face was puzzled. "She doesn't really believe that I am Elvis Presley, does she?"

Meghan shook her head. "I don't know," she replied. "Earl, what are you doing all dressed up in that outfit? Are you taking over your uncle's business? What's going on?"

He blushed. "I hoped I wouldn't run into anyone I knew," he said sheepishly. "But I'm running out of money, and my uncle's costumes are all sitting in my apartment... I went to the manager of the Venetian and talked with her, and she agreed to let me take over his role. I need to pay the bills somehow, and I know what to do, so it seemed like a perfect fit."

Meghan smiled. "That's amazing," she told him. "I'm glad to hear one tidbit of good news today!"

He nodded. "I'm starting to really enjoy it," he admitted, his eyes bright. "Something inside of me thinks perhaps I was born for the stage. I really get a rush when I perform!"

Before she could respond, she felt a tap on her shoulder. "Excuse me?"

She turned to find a red-headed man with a large mustache staring at her. “Are you Meghan Truman?”

“Yes… who is asking?” she replied to the stranger.

He revealed a manilla envelope from his briefcase.

“This is for you.”

“What is it?” she asked in confusion. “And how did you find me?”

“I have my ways,” he told her ominously. “This is a subpoena from the attorney of Louise Wilson. Mrs. Wilson, the wife of the late Jeremiah Wilson, is *suing* you in civil court for the death of her husband.”

13

Earl's eyes widened. "Yikes. That sounds rough. On that note, I had better get back to the theater! See you later."

Meghan's mouth fell open in disbelief. "Are you kidding?" she exclaimed as the lawyer handed her the documents. "After everything I've been through on this stupid trip, Louise Wilson is suing me in civil court?"

Jackie and Karen walked into the lobby just as Meghan insulted the bachelorette weekend. "Stupid trip? Gee thanks, Meghan. It's not like *anyone* put a lot of hard work into making this a great time for you."

Meghan turned to face her. "Don't you start with me! This trip has been all about you. You know I never wanted to come to Vegas, and yet, here we are in a

dumpy motel with a lawyer telling me I'm getting sued for someone's death?"

Jackie tightened her left hand into a fist. "Don't you act like this is my fault."

"I would say it is your fault," Myrtle chimed in as she came back to the lobby. "We told you that Meghan wanted a quiet trip."

"She's right," Karen added. "When you told us about Vegas, I told you that Meghan would hate it and that she would even prefer staying in Sandy Bay and doing a little girls' weekend."

Jackie scowled. "I wanted to make it special."

Meghan shook her head. "You wanted to make it something *you* would find special. This isn't me, and you know it."

Belinda scurried over to the group. "You ladies are causing a scene! Stop shouting at once!"

Todd appeared, and he shooed Belinda away. "I'll take care of them, Belinda. What's wrong, Meghan? Did something happen? I've heard your group has had a rough time with all the news crews outside…"

Meghan could feel her face growing hot. "A rough time doesn't even begin to describe it," she told him. "I need to take matters into my own hands."

"What do you mean?" he asked.

"Can you take me to the theater at The Venetian? I

need to get over there and figure out just how this mess started."

He nodded. "No problem. I'm still on the clock, but I can leave in thirty minutes if that's ok?"

She agreed, and then turned to her friends. "I am going to get to the bottom of all of this. I didn't have anything to do with Jeremiah's death, but unless I prove that, the police won't let us leave Las Vegas. I am going to the theater and solving this mystery!"

An hour later, Todd and Meghan arrived at The Venetian. The theater was empty except for Earl, who was practicing his set on stage. "Hey Meghan!" he greeted as she followed Todd inside. "Hope everything got figured out for you."

He returned to his set, and Meghan turned to Todd. "Thanks for bringing me down here."

"Not a problem," he assured her. "I'm happy to help. I know quite a few people around The Venetian, so it wasn't hard getting you in to peek around."

Meghan raised an eyebrow. "You have such a way with people," she told him. "My group of friends has really taken to you, and the receptionist here nearly swooned when you walked in."

He laughed. "I've always been a people person," he

said. "That's why I got into hospitality in the first place."

Todd led Meghan into the first row of seats. She

stared around the massive theater, in awe of its enormity. "This place is huge," she commented. "I can't believe Earl gets to play here as the new Elvis."

"He's a lucky guy," Todd replied. "Playing Elvis in Las Vegas is a lucrative situation. Earl is going to make more money than he knows what to do with."

"You think so?"

"Absolutely," he nodded. "From what his uncle used to say when he'd hung around the hotel bar, he took home a five-figure salary each month. That isn't too bad for a guy who plays a few songs and wiggles his hips for middle-aged female tourists."

Meghan giggled as she imagined Mrs. Sheridan throwing herself at Jeremiah. "The Elvis gig does seem to get a lot of attention," she agreed. "You said Jeremiah would hang around the bar? Did you know him well?"

Todd shook his head. "He came around the bar a lot, but I wouldn't say we were friends. It's sad he passed away, though; he was well known around the city, and I feel bad for his wife."

"What do you think about the new Elvis?" she asked as she pointed to Earl. "He's a nice guy. He's Jeremiah's nephew; did you know that?"

"His nephew?" Todd asked. "I didn't realize that. Lucky guy, though. Getting a role like that as a young guy is a big deal... it took Jeremiah *years* to earn a spot playing here as Elvis. That nephew of his is

lucky, lucky, lucky!"

Meghan nodded. "I wouldn't mind making that kind of money, and I'm gonna need it if I'm dragged into court with this civil suit. Let's start looking around here; I want to tear this place apart and see if I can find any clues."

They spent the next hour poking around the theater. "I don't see anything," Todd called out to her from across the room. "Everything looks normal."

She sighed. Todd was right; nothing was amiss in the theater, and she still had no idea how Jeremiah had died. "Let's just call it a day."

Earl was still practicing his set as they left the theater, and Meghan could hear his voice as they walked into a long hallway. "Do you want to see something cool?" Todd asked.

"Sure," she nodded as he led her into a dark room.

He flipped on the lights. "Ta-da!"

She gasped. The room was filled with mannequins wearing different versions of Elvis costumes. The outfits represented his early career, mannequins dressed in jumpsuits, and an entire shelf filled with accessories and wigs. "What is this?"

"This is the costume room," he explained as he took a wig from the shelf and placed it on Meghan's head. "Isn't it neat?"

She nodded. "This is one of the coolest things I've

seen in Vegas," she admitted as she spotted a white jumpsuit with red and blue sequins. "That costume is incredible!"

"Try it on," Todd urged. "I'll snap a photo of you in it. You can send it to your man!"

She smiled and took the costume off of its hanger. "There is some cushion in the backside and stomach area," he warned as she tried to snap herself into it. "Those were from Elvis' fat days. For some reason, the outfits from his fatter years are the most popular."

She buttoned the top buttons and looked into the floor-length mirror in the corner. "With this wig on, I could pass for the King," she joked as she turned to look at her backside. "This *is* a lot of cushion!"

The door opened, and a uniformed theater attendant came inside. "Play it cool," Todd whispered to her. "We really shouldn't be in here…"

"Earl?" the man asked as he locked eyes with Meghan. "Your show begins soon."

Meghan shook her head. "Ummm... okay, thank you," she replied, trying to make her voice sound gruff.

"Do you want your water on the stage or in your

dressing room?" he asked.

"Both," she answered. "Please."

He peered at her. "That's different from your usual," he said. "But ok…"

Todd smiled. "Earl will be out in a few minutes," he said as he put a hand on the attendant's shoulder and led him to the door. "Thanks."

Meghan sighed as he left. "He really thought I was Earl," she remarked.

"The costume is really convincing," he laughed. "Let's get you out of here.

Meghan removed the costume, and they returned to the hallway.

"Hey! Hey! Meghan Truman?" a girl's voice cried, and they turned around.

"Please don't be another attorney," she prayed silently. She was relieved when she found it was a teenage girl.

"Can I help you?" she asked.

"Can I get an autograph and a photo?" the girl asked, her eyes dancing with excitement.

"With me?" Meghan asked. "What for?"

"You're that girl!" the teenager cried. "The girl on the

news! I want an autograph with the girl who was having an affair with Elvis! Pretty please? Maybe a photo too?!"

14

Todd shooed the girl away. "You're being quite rude! Get out of here!"

Meghan wanted to tear her hair out in frustration. "I don't understand," she lamented as they walked out of The Venetian and into the bright afternoon sunshine. "I didn't even know Jeremiah Wilson! Why does everyone think I had something to do with him *dying*? It's terrible!"

Todd shook his head. "I'm sorry," he told her. "I wish I could do something to help."

She frowned. "I need to get back to the hotel. Thanks for bringing me over here."

He gave her a dramatic bow. "Of course, m'lady! Not a problem in the slightest. Let me know if there is ever anything else I can do."

They said goodbye, and she booked a taxi on her Uber app which she took back to the hotel. Upon her arrival, she was pleased to find that the crowd of reporters had vanished. A police officer was stationed outside the hotel, and she had to flash her ID before entering. "New protocol," he told her gruffly as she showed him her driver's license. "The press was getting to be too much, so the manager insisted we post an officer outside to check guest IDs."

"That's a good idea," Meghan told him, thankful she didn't have to wade through an ocean of press.

When she entered the lobby, she saw it was empty, and felt relieved; she was tired, homesick, and frustrated, and the last thing she wanted to deal with was her group of friends. Meghan sat down on a lumpy maroon couch and checked her cell phone for any new messages.

"Excuse me?"

She groaned as a tall man in a suit approached her. "Yes?"

"Are you Meghan Truman?"

She nearly laughed. Could she not have just one second alone?

"Maybe," she answered cautiously. "And who are you?"

"I'm Ryan Heeber," he told her. "I'm an attorney for Louise Wilson."

She moaned aloud, burying her face in her hands. "Is something wrong?" he asked.

She shook her head. "Why can't Louise just leave me alone?"

Ryan chuckled. "That's why I am here," he informed her. "I have come over to propose a settlement. Mrs. Wilson wants nothing more to do with you, and she would like to end all of this trouble right now."

Meghan's ears perked up. "She's done? Really? She wants to leave me alone?"

Ryan nodded. "Yes, she does. If you sign this paper, then it will all be over."

He shoved an envelope in her face, along with a pen, and Meghan peered at the fine print. "This is a settlement document," she said to herself. "Wait... she doesn't want to end things. She wants me to settle with her for the death of her husband!"

Ryan nodded. He had a weak chin and white blonde eyebrows, and Meghan could sense that she couldn't trust him. "That's what I meant," he explained, a smile creeping onto his face. "She wants you to pay her out, and then all of this will go away. You can go home to Sandy Bay, you can leave Vegas, and you can have your life back. What do you say?"

Meghan stared at the paperwork. "She wants to settle

for 3.5 million dollars!" she exclaimed. "I don't have that kind of money; I run a small bakery. How does she expect me to pay that?"

The lawyer shrugged. "That's not her concern," he told her. "But... my client is aware of some family money you might have access to. When we looked into your background, we found that your father, Henry Truman, could help you out…"

Meghan gasped. "You looked into my family?"

"Of course," he replied. "We needed to know the full story. It sounds like your daddy has had some legal problems of his own, so it's not a surprise that his daughter is running wild in Vegas and causing the death of a sweet woman's husband…"

Meghan crossed her arms over her chest, rising from her chair and staring Ryan Heeber in the eyes. "You need to leave," she said coldly. "You have no business being here. I'm not paying your client a cent, and you can tell her that!"

The attorney rolled his eyes. "She worried you might have a strong reaction," he told her. "I'll leave, but don't forget, we're watching you."

She glared at him. "If you don't leave now, I am going to fetch that police officer! You don't belong here."

He winked. "Or do I? Here. Take my card. You're going to need it."

He handed Meghan a thick silver business card and left the hotel. She collapsed into a chair, tears pouring down her face. How had things gone awry in such a hideous fashion? She knew she couldn't afford to pay

out Mrs. Wilson, and she knew she was innocent. She was going to have to get to the bottom of Jeremiah's death whether she liked it or not.

She sat alone downstairs for awhile, enjoying the solitude. Her heart sank as she spotted Jackie coming down the stairs, and she tried to hide her face under her thick hair.

"I can see you are trying to hide from me," Jackie called her out. "We have a problem."

Meghan narrowed her eyes at her friend. "Another problem? Shocker."

Jackie put her hands on her hips. "Don't give me attitude right now, Meghan! We have a serious problem, and we need your help."

"You always need my help," Meghan complained. "In Sandy Bay, here in Vegas... where does it end?"

Jackie shook her head. "I am going to ignore your snarky comments," she said evenly. "Because we have bigger fish to fry."

"What do you mean?"

The rest of the ladies rushed into the room. "Meghan!" Karen cried. "We need to talk to you!"

Before Meghan could say anything, a woman ran to the group. “Excuse me,” the woman began. “Meghan Truman? Is that you?”

“It is,” Jackie confirmed. “She’s THE Meghan

Truman! Would you like to buy a t-shirt with her face on it? I will cut you a deal, too. I’ll give you the t-shirt and a photo with Meghan for two-hundred bucks.”

Meghan gasped. “Jackie! Seriously? Cut it out.”

“I’ll take it!” the woman agreed. “A photo and t-shirt of the woman who killed Elvis? My friends from my book club won’t believe it. We all love mystery books and television shows, and now, I’m here with a real-life villain!”

Trudy glowered at the woman. “Get out of here,” she ordered. “You are invading our privacy.”

“But she said…” the woman argued as she pointed to Jackie. “She said I could have…”

“I don’t care what she said,” Trudy countered. “Get out of here or I will call the police!”

The woman frowned, but she scurried away.

“What is going on?” Meghan asked. “Seriously. What do you all need?”

Before anyone else could answer, Jackie took a deep breath. “I hate to be the one to tell you this, but Mrs.

Sheridan has disappeared."

15

"What?" Meghan gasped. "Disappeared?"

"No one has seen her in hours," Jackie confirmed. "Myrtle and Trudy took her to her room earlier, and now, no one can find her."

"Has anyone at the hotel seen her?"

"No one," Jackie answered. "We need to search for her; I'm worried that she went looking for Elvis, and who knows where she could end up!"

They assembled the women in the lobby. "We need to split up and search for her," Meghan told the group. "We don't know where she could be, or who she could be with, so we can't leave a single stone unturned!"

"I'll go with you," Myrtle told her. "Everyone else

spread out and search the Strip; we need to find her quickly!"

The women left the hotel. They stopped to buy hot dogs from a vendor, and continued on their search. As they walked along the busy strip, Meghan was deep in her thoughts. She could feel her heart beating rapidly in her chest; what if something terrible had happened to Mrs. Sheridan? How could she return to Sandy Bay without her friend?

"It is really cool here," Myrtle commented as they passed the Hard Rock Cafe. "The lights are so bright, and it is so busy."

"Mama would hate it here," Meghan laughed as they passed a group of scantily clad dancers performing on the street corner. "She would think it is so tacky."

Myrtle giggled. "She would turn up her fancy nose in a heartbeat."

"Not only at this city, but at us right now," Meghan giggled. "Hot dogs? You know Mama would not approve."

"It's common fair food," Myrtle said, imitating their mother. "Truman girls don't eat fair food!"

They continued to walk along the strip, each looking left and right for Mrs. Sheridan.

"How are you doing?" Myrtle asked her as they

crossed the street. "I know it hasn't been the trip of your dreams, but have there been any good parts?"

Meghan pursed her lips. She knew Myrtle meant well, but she didn't want to answer her sister's question. "Meghan?" Myrtle pressed.

"I'm hanging in there," she told her sister. "I'm glad you are here. You've been my saving grace."

"Happy to help, sis."

Meghan's heart warmed as she thought of how much she loved her sister. "This is a little unceremonious," she admitted. "But can I ask you a question? It's important."

"Sure," Myrtle agreed. "What's up?"

Meghan reached for her sister's hand and gave it a squeeze. "You're my closest sister and one of my best friends," she began. "Would you be my maid of honor? I would be so happy if you'd say yes."

"YES!" Myrtle squealed. "Of course! I was hoping you would ask me!"

Meghan beamed. "That makes me so happy," she told her sister. "Mama has really gone crazy with the wedding planning; she wants three string quartets, a petting zoo for the children in attendance, a choreographed Viennese waltz for our first dance, and a fountain built for the reception. I need someone level-headed to keep me grounded during my big day, and I couldn't think of anyone better than my favorite sister."

Myrtle jumped up and down with joy. "I thought you would never ask. Who else do you think will be in the

bridal party?"

"Our sisters, of course," Meghan answered. "Karen, Trudy, Pamela, and Jackie."

"Jackie?" Myrtle asked. "Are you sure? The way this trip has gone, I wouldn't be surprised if you never wanted to see her stupid face again."

Meghan sighed. "She is my friend," she explained. "And even though this weekend has gone awry, I don't want to lose a friend."

Myrtle rolled her eyes. "You're too kind," she told her. "I would kick her out of my life if she planned a trip like this for me."

Meghan shook her head. "I don't believe in being vindictive," she said to her younger sister. "I hope this whole situation with Jackie is just a fluke and that I can still enjoy her company on my wedding day."

They reached the next corner, and Meghan was nearly flattened as a group of Asian tourists walked in her direction. "Hey!" she shouted as a man almost hit her in the face with his giant camera. "I'm walking here."

The group of tourists did not move, and Meghan got caught up in the middle of them. A young girl wearing a pair of aviator sunglasses and a Minnie

Mouse backpack pointed at Meghan. She yelled over her shoulder to the group, and Meghan could not understand what she was saying.

Myrtle edged her way into the group. "They swept you up," she commented in amusement. "This tour group is huge."

"Let's try to get out of here," Meghan said, feeling frazzled as the tourists bumped into her. The girl with the sunglasses pointed at her again.

"That's Meghan Truman! She had an affair with Elvis!"

Meghan's stomach sank as the tourists turned to her and began to take photos. "Meghan! Take a photo with me!" they asked as they shoved their cell phones and cameras in her face.

"Meghan! Take my hand!" Myrtle shouted as a child with a cell phone climbed on Meghan's back and began to pose for photos.

Meghan reached out and took her sister's hand, and Myrtle pushed through the crowd to break free of the tourists. "Meghan! There she goes!" they yelled, but Meghan and Myrtle were sprinting down the street.

"This is the worst weekend of my life!" Meghan screamed in frustration. "This mess is the last thing I expected on my special trip; why did all of this have to happen to me?"

Before Myrtle could answer, a man in a three-piece

suit sauntered up to Meghan. "Excuse my interruption," he said smoothly as he pushed his blonde hair back. "Did I hear correctly? Are you Meghan Truman?"

She bit her lip and shook her head. "No," she lied. "I'm not."

He winked at her. "Don't be silly; I recognize you from the news footage. I think this chance meeting is exactly what you need, Meghan. I'm Patrick Jackson, Attorney."

She groaned. "Another attorney? Who are you working for? Louise? How many attorneys does that woman need?"

He laughed. "I'm not working for Louise Wilson," he assured her as Myrtle eyed him suspiciously. "I want to be working for *you*; I'm new in town, and I need to establish a reputation, and after looking into your case, I think I can get you out of the mess you're in."

"Really?" she asked. "How?"

"I looked into Louise Wilson, and she has quite a rap sheet," he informed her. "There are things about her that you should know, and I think I can leverage those things to get you out of this city faster than you can say Sin City."

Myrtle raised an eyebrow. "We'll think about it," she told him. "Do you have a business card?"

He nodded, pulling a card from his jacket and

handing it to Meghan. "Call *any* time. I look forward to hearing from you."

16

"He has never looked more handsome," Meghan thought as she stared at Jack.

Jack was dressed in a tuxedo. His blonde hair slicked back into the same style that Patrick Johnson's hair had been during their encounter. He had a smile on his face, and Meghan saw there was a corsage of baby's breath pinned to his jacket. Her mother adored baby's breath, and even though Meghan had not wanted to use the flower in the corsages, she was happy that her mother had insisted.

Meghan watched as Jack walked up to a large white gazebo that was covered in lilies. Her parents had constructed the gazebo, especially for the wedding, and she knew it would look beautiful in photos. The photographer had already made her pose by the new structure earlier that day, snapping photo after photo of Meghan beaming in her gown.

Her dress was like a work of art; Mama's French seamstress had designed the white satin ballgown, and it made Meghan look like a princess. The sweetheart neckline was trimmed with pearls, and the skirt fell in a way that made Meghan appear elegant. The sleeves were puffed, and each one resembled a perfectly crafted snowball. Meghan's hair was pulled up into a high up-do, and her dark hair was cradled by a snood studded with pearls that matched her dress.

She gasped as the music began to play; it was Canon in D, the song typically rendered as brides walked down the aisle. It was time to be married to her handsome groom!

She looked down, her heart beating in her chest as her father took her elbow and nodded, but instead of guiding her forward, they did not move. She tried to move her feet, but it was as if she were glued to the ground. "Daddy?"

Her father shrugged. "Daddy, it's our turn," she told him as the crowd stood up.

Her father said nothing. Meghan couldn't move, and she gasped as another woman in a white dress pushed past her and began to walk toward Jack. Her eyes nearly fell out of her head; the bride was Mrs. Sheridan! She was dressed in an old-fashioned wedding dress with puff sleeves, a high neckline, and a floppy white lace hat and matching cane.

"What is going on?" Meghan asked her father as Mrs. Sheridan floated down the aisle toward *her* fiancé.

Mrs. Sheridan reached Jack, and they took hands. Karen appeared beside them; she was holding a Bible, and dressed in a minister's outfit. "Karen?" Meghan wondered. "What is going on here?"

"We are gathered here today…." Karen began as Meghan's dark eyes widened.

"He's leaving me for Sally Sheridan? I don't understand! What is going on?" she lamented as she watched Jack read vows to Mrs. Sheridan.

"Daddy? Daddy?"

Her father said nothing. She broke free from her father. She ran down the aisle and stood between them, but no one could see her. "Hey! Hey! Jack is mine!" she insisted, but no one responded to her. It was as if she were invisible.

"Hey! Hey! Stop! He's with me!" she screamed to no avail.

Meghan woke up in a panic, her skin cold and sweaty as she gasped for breath. The entire miserable scene had been a nightmare, and she tried to catch her breath. "What a terrible dream," she muttered as she reached over and grabbed her cell phone from the bedside table. Though she had felt like she had been asleep for hours, she had only been dreaming for about twenty minutes.

"That was ridiculous," she murmured as she read through her messages. "Jack would never leave me for her."

As she glanced through her phone, it began to ring. It was a number she did not recognize, but she answered it anyway. "Meghan Truman speaking."

"Meghan? This is Officer Brady."

She groaned as she remembered the long night she had spent in jail. "How can I help you?"

"We've almost finished the autopsy," he informed her. "And we can confidently report that the bite of your pie that Jeremiah took did not kill him."

"That's great!" she cried. "So I am not a suspect anymore? I can go back to Sandy Bay?"

"Not quite," he told her. "We are still conducting tests on the scene, and we have a few more tests to perform on the body. We need you to remain in the area for further questioning."

"More questioning?" she asked, her heart heavy with the news that she would have to remain in Las Vegas even longer. "Why?"

Officer Brady scoffed. "Because I said so; I've seen the news reports and realize that your relationship with Mr. Wilson seems to be more complicated than you led us to believe. You must comply with our instructions or you will find yourself back in jail."

"Relationship?" she shrieked. "I didn't even know him! Don't believe what you see on the news. Is this a bad joke?"

"This is not a joke," he said gruffly. "Do what we ask

of you, or else."

He hung up the phone, and she moaned. All Meghan wanted to do was get home to Jack and her business, and she could hardly stand being in Las Vegas for another minute.

There was a knock at the door, causing her to jump in panic. Who could be at her door at this hour? She got up and reached for a clothing hanger, hoping she could use it as a weapon if someone dangerous were at the door.

"Who is it?" she asked anxiously.

"Mr. Elway, the owner of the hotel. Please open the door."

She opened the door to find Lucky Elway staring at her. "I'm sorry to bother you this late," he apologized. "But I've been watching the news, and I think we need to talk."

She frowned. "Don't believe everything you see on the news," she muttered as she stared at her bare feet.

"I don't," he assured her. "In fact, I think the claims against you are ridiculous. But, as a business owner, I want to capitalize on what's going on. Do you get what I'm saying?"

"No," she told him. "What do you mean?"

"Our website crashed," he said. "We had over a million people try to access our website today. My investors called, as well as the CEO of the Vegas

Tourism Board, and they had great news for me."

"What does this have to do with me?"

"Because everyone in this city wants to see the hotel where Elvis' killer stayed," he grinned. "The CEO of the Tourism Board wants to add our hotel to a number of tours. They want to feature the hotel on the city and state tourism website. We are going to make so much money from all of this!"

Meghan furrowed her brow. "That's insane," she told him. "I didn't kill Jeremiah Wilson, and anyone who knows anything about his death should understand that! It doesn't seem fair to me that you are going to profit off of my misfortune."

Lucky shrugged. "That's why I am here. You've helped elevate my hotel to a level I didn't realize was possible, and I want to do something nice for you! I've spoken to Belinda and Todd, and we want to upgrade your stay here."

"An upgrade?"

"To our Queen Suite," he announced grandly. "Pack your things, and I will take you up there now. It's our finest room; the decor is new, the furniture is comfortable, and we think you will enjoy it!"

Meghan gathered her belongings and followed Lucky into the hallway. "You'll be even more comfortable in the Queen Suite," he assured her as he led her down the hall. "Here we are!"

They arrived in front of a pink door. Lucky threw it

open. "Ta-da!"

She looked around. The room was exactly the same as her previous room, the difference being a small couch in the corner and a mini-fridge next to the bed.

"What do you think?" he grinned at her. "Isn't it magical?"

She stifled a laugh; the situation was becoming funnier by the second, and she wondered if Lucky truly believed the room was better, or if he was just pulling her leg.

"It's GREAT," she complimented sarcastically. "Gorgeous. Magnificent. It's so different than my last room."

"I'm glad you think so," he said earnestly as he took her bags and placed them on the bed. "I hope you enjoy it. We will also be assuming the cost of the rest of your stay here. You have brought us so much attention, and we can't thank you enough!"

Lucky bid her a good night and left the room. She

began to unpack her bags, and as she pulled her wallet out of her purse, a thick business card fell out. She picked it up. It was the card from Patrick Jackson, the attorney she had met earlier.

Meghan took a deep breath and pulled out her phone. She dialed the number, holding her breath as the call began to go through.

17

"Hello?" Patrick Jackson answered sleepily. "Who is this?"

"It's Meghan Truman," she told him as she clutched the phone to her ear. "I'm sorry to call so late, but I've thought about what you said, and I think that I could use you on my side."

"That's great," he replied. "I'm happy to hear that."

"I want to visit Louise Wilson's lawyer and see if we can work something out," she said. "I want to go down there by myself and talk it out with the lawyer; I can be very persuasive, and I am not afraid to stand up for myself."

Patrick snorted. "That is a terrible idea," he said. "Meghan, you're not playing with small-town lawyers from Sandy Bay; Louise Wilson is cut-throat,

and from what I've researched about her lawyers, they are, too."

"Then what do you suggest?"

"Meet me," he told her. "Meet me at Soma, the coffee shop around the corner from your hotel. I'll be there in twenty minutes, and from there, we'll go to her lawyer's house."

He hung up the phone, and Meghan quickly called Karen. She knew Karen would be the right person to support her during her conversation with Patrick, and she hoped her friend wasn't asleep already.

"Hello? Meghan?"

"I'm so glad you answered," she said. "I'm going to work with an attorney to get us out of this situation," she explained. "He wants to meet with me in twenty minutes. Will you come?"

"In twenty minutes? But it's almost nine at night," Karen replied. "Are you sure it's a good idea?"

"I don't have a lot of options," Meghan lamented. "He offered to take on my case, and I need all the help I can get. Please? Come with me?"

Karen sighed. "You know I need my full nine hours of sleep," Karen answered. "But for you, of course, I will help."

They met up with Patrick. As they left the coffee shop, several tourists pulled their phones out and began taking photos of Meghan. "It's Meghan

Truman! There she is!"

"Why is she out so late?" one of the tourists asked. "It's nine at night! Nothing good happens after nine."

"She's with a man! Is that your new boyfriend?" another tourist asked.

Patrick shook his head and showed Meghan and Karen to his car.

"This isn't what I expected a lawyer to drive," Karen commented as she surveyed his vehicle. The interior was spotless, but the outside had clearly seen better days.

"It's a used car," he admitted. "I'm new in town, and I'm not making the big bucks yet."

They sped off in the night, leaving the lights and glamour of the city and heading to the suburbs. "Is it a far drive?" Meghan asked.

"Not too far," he assured her. "Her lawyer, Pete Lawrence, lives out in one of the fancy neighborhoods just north of the city. We'll be there in twenty minutes or so."

They were quiet on the drive, and while Meghan was tired, she could feel her adrenaline rushing. She was eager to confront Louise's attorney, and though she was nervous about showing up at his home in the middle of the night, she was hopeful that Patrick Jackson would help her.

Patrick drove them into a neighborhood filled with magnificent homes. “This is so nice,” Karen admired as they passed a massive stucco house with a large fence out front. “Louise must be paying him well.”

Patrick chuckled. “You wouldn’t believe how much…”

They pulled into a long drive. “Is this it?” Meghan asked as she stared at a three-story stucco house with a grand fountain in the front. “The lights are on. Is he expecting us at this hour?”

“He shouldn’t be,” Patrick told her. “I didn’t call ahead. Maybe he’s a night owl?”

They climbed out of the car, and Karen led the way to the front door. She knocked, but no one answered. “What now?”

Patrick knocked even louder, but no one came to the door. “We could keep knocking or go home,” he shrugged. “We can’t break and enter.”

“Oh, yes we can!” Meghan declared as she gently turned the doorknob and found it was open. “I didn’t come all the way out here for nothing.”

She quietly opened the door and walked inside, Karen and Patrick following along behind her. “Shhh,” she told them. “Maybe he isn’t home, maybe he is, but either way, we want to find, not be found."

They walked into a large entryway. Tasteful prints of southwestern art hung on the walls, and a red fringe rug lay across the tiled floor. "I like his style," Karen commented quietly. "Great prints."

Meghan led them to a door that was closed. "I wonder what's in here," she thought aloud. "A closed door on the first floor... maybe this is his office?"

She carefully turned the handle and walked inside, gasping as she recognized the room's occupants. She, Karen, and Patrick all raised their eyebrows.

"What is going on in here?" Meghan cried as she saw Pete Lawrence and Louise Wilson sitting together on a red leather couch, their limbs intertwined and their faces flushed.

"What is this?" Pete yelled. "What are you doing in my house?"

Louise screamed. "Call the police!"

Karen pulled out her phone and snapped a picture of the pair. "Not so fast," she warned them. "What are you two doing together? Louise, your husband just *died*, and you're all cozied up with the attorney that's trying to pin your husband's death on my friend? I don't think so."

Karen took several pictures. "I've emailed those photos to myself," she declared, her head held high. "And I am going to forward them to the police if you don't answer our questions."

Louise frowned. "You don't have anything on us; we are simply talking about legal matters."

"That's not what it looks like," Meghan scoffed.

Patrick crossed his arms over his chest. "I've done a

background check on Louise," he announced as Pete glared at him.

"*Who* are you?" Pete asked.

"I'm Meghan's attorney," Patrick informed him. "And as I was saying, my background check on Louise yielded some interesting results; Mrs. Wilson has been married three times, and coincidentally, all three of her ex-husbands were either declared bankrupt or had fatal accidents. Louise has received over sixteen million dollars from the deaths and divorce settlements of these former husbands, and I'm wondering if Jeremiah Wilson might be her latest victim."

Louise scowled. "I loved Jeremiah," she spat at Patrick. "How dare you? Jeremiah had nothing; he walked into this marriage empty-handed, and I loved him for who he was."

Patrick adjusted his tie with an attitude that made Meghan laugh to herself. "He may have walked in with nothing," he told Louise. "But you and I both know that he didn't die with nothing; that gig at The

Venetian was a massive deal for him, and his net worth was estimated at 3.5 million dollars when he died."

Louise glared at him. "That's none of your business."

"Oh, but it is," Patrick continued. "And I happened to find documentation that states you filed for divorce from Jeremiah only months before his death. It was approved the day he died. Did you know that?"

She shook her head. "We reconciled," she shrugged. "I loved him."

Patrick rolled his eyes. "Legally, at the time of his death, Jeremiah wasn't your husband. Your case is bogus, Louise, and you know it. Pete, you know it too. In fact, you and I also know that it is out of line for you to have a relationship with your client. We have evidence that could get you disbarred."

Pete balled his hands into fists. "What do you want, Paul?"

"Patrick," he corrected. "I want you to drop the case against my client, or I am forwarding those pictures to the state bar association."

Pete clenched his jaw. "Get out of my house," he demanded. "And just so you know, even if we drop this case, your client, Meghan Truman, is still a suspect! I have evidence to prove it."

"Oh yeah?" Meghan countered. "Like what?"

Before Pete could answer, the door to the office opened, and a stout woman walked into the room. "What is going on here? Honey?"

Pete rose from the couch and straightened his tie. "Hi dear," he greeted the woman, kissing her on the cheek. "How are you? You are back early from your trip!"

"The kids wanted to see their dad," she said. "And I missed my husband."

Louise tried to straighten her hair, but the woman caught sight of her. "Mrs. Wilson? What are you doing over here so late? You look flushed! And these others? What is going on here?"

"I think it's our time to go," Meghan whispered to Karen and Patrick. "It looks like Pete has some dirty little secrets of his own, and I don't want to be around for this fight!"

18

"Patrick?" Meghan said as he drove them back to the hotel. "Why are you helping us?"
"Exposure," he answered. "I need my name out there. I've told you that."
She raised an eyebrow. "Come on," she urged him. "I have a sense that there's something else…"
"Okay," he smiled. "You're intuitive, aren't you? Okay, okay, you are right. I am helping you for more than exposure."

"Do tell," Karen told him.

"My dad was a gambling addict," he began. "He was a doctor, but because of his problems, he spent all of our family's money on his addiction, and after we lost our house, he took his own life. I was nineteen at that time, but my mom had six other kids to feed. We were broke, and my mom didn't have a job, so I had to become the breadwinner for all eight of us."

"I am so sorry," Meghan said softly. "How terrible that must have been."

"It was hard," he agreed. "And my father's debts ran a lot deeper than we realized. He was involved with the Brazilian drug cartel, and those debts are almost endless."

Karen clasped a hand over her mouth. "This is crazy…"

He shrugged. "I have to pay off my father's debts, or my family will be in danger. I went to law school to become a lawyer and earn the big bucks, and by my projections, I should have this debt paid off in the next five or ten years."

"That's amazing!" Meghan told him. "You are a hero for your family."

"I try my best," he said softly. "When I saw the footage of Meghan hounded by reporters, it reminded me of my poor mom. When my dad died by suicide, we were swamped by reporters. He was a prominent person in the medical community, and the reporters harassed my mom to no end. It made me sick. Meghan, you have an innocent look in your eyes, and from the moment I saw the videos, I knew I wanted to help you."

Meghan smiled. "You are too kind," she told him.

"And brave and good. Your family must be so proud of you."

He grinned. "They are," he agreed. "But I am just blessed to have them."

Patrick dropped them off at the hotel, but Meghan was too excited to sleep. "Can you believe it?" she asked Karen, her eyes bright. "They have to drop their case against me. They can't extort me!"

Karen bit her lip. "I'm nervous about what he said about the evidence against you," she told Meghan.

"I think he was bluffing," Meghan said. "Let's talk more about it over some food; I'm starving, and this is the first time I've really been hungry all weekend."

They walked down the block to a diner. Meghan looked around, and seeing no tourists, she felt comfortable going in and sitting down. They ordered waffles, sausage, pancakes, and toast, and she was thrilled when the waitress didn't recognize her.

"Who do you think killed Jeremiah?" Karen asked. "Or do you think anyone killed him? Maybe it was a total accident. He wasn't a spring chicken, that's for sure."

Meghan dug into her pancakes, thinking as she savored its flavor. "I think it was Louise," she replied. "She is a fancy woman with fancy taste, and Jeremiah was common and tacky. I'm sure she hated him, and I bet she thought she could walk away with more of his money if he died rather than if she divorced him."

"That's what I think, too," Karen agreed. "Tonight confirmed it all; Louise killed him, but she's going to use her fancy-pants lawyer boyfriend to cover it all up."

Meghan frowned. "It's unfair how rich people can use their money to get out of trouble," she sighed.

Karen nodded, but then, Meghan saw her eyes turn to the left. "Hey, isn't that Mrs. Sheridan?" Karen asked as they both turned to glance at a woman sitting alone a few booths away.

Meghan squinted her eyes and gasped. "It is! That's her! Oh, thank goodness she is okay!"

Karen stood up. "Let's go talk to her," she suggested.

Meghan raised a finger to her lips. "She's been acting so weird here," she whispered. "Let's just follow her; we don't know what she's been up to, and we don't want her to freak out here at the diner."

They watched Mrs. Sheridan for awhile, and when she got up, they stood up as well. "Let's follow her," Meghan whispered to Karen. "Come on! She's leaving."

They followed Mrs. Sheridan outside and down the block. Meghan prayed that no one would recognize her; it was nearly two in the morning after all.

Mrs. Sheridan entered a souvenir shop just around the corner from the diner. "Make sure she doesn't see you," Meghan cautioned Karen. "We don't want her to call attention to us."

Karen nodded. They watched as Mrs. Sheridan browsed a rack of sunglasses, a case of t-shirts, and a stack of flip-flops. She didn't purchase anything, and she walked out of the shop empty-handed.

Her next stop was a costume shop. Meghan and Karen followed behind her, and they carefully walked into the store. Karen laughed as Mrs. Sheridan pulled a witch hat off of a display and tried it on. "She's wearing the clothes she was meant to wear," Karen joked.

"You're so bad," Meghan admonished as they watched Mrs. Sheridan remove the hat from her head and replace it with a tiara. "That's her real look; Queen Sheridan is here!"

Mrs. Sheridan removed the tiara and moved on to the next display. She selected a green wig from a rack. Meghan decided it was time to confront her; she was tired, and it was time to get Mrs. Sheridan back to the hotel.

She tip-toed over and snatched the wig off of her head. "Mrs. Sheridan!" she cried.

She was shocked when she turned around; the woman was not Mrs. Sheridan, but rather, a complete stranger.

"Who are you?" the woman cried as Meghan gasped. "I know who you are! You are the woman who killed Elvis!"

Meghan shook her head. "No! I didn't have anything

to do with that. Please don't scream. I can explain…"

The stranger's eyes widened. "I knew you were following me!" she shouted. "You're going to kill me like you killed Elvis! Help! Help!"

Meghan looked at Karen and mouthed, "run". The two women bolted from the store, Meghan trying to keep up with Karen as they dashed through the street.

"I hear sirens!" Karen told her as they rounded a corner. "She must have called the police."

"Run faster!" Meghan cried, and they took off down an unfamiliar street.

The sirens grew closer, and Meghan felt out of breath as they turned another corner. "Are we almost back?" she asked Karen as they dodged a group of street entertainers.

"I don't know," Karen told her. "I think we're lost…"

19

It was five in the morning by the time they finally reached the hotel. Meghan and Karen were filthy from hours of wandering the streets of Las Vegas, and they collapsed onto a couch in the lobby.

"Do you think Mrs. Sheridan is back yet?" Karen asked.

"The real one? Or the one I scared?" Meghan joked darkly.

"The real one," Karen said. "Let's go ask Belinda if she's back. Maybe she's seen her?"

They went up to the desk to find Belinda flipping through a clothing catalog. "What?" she asked rudely. "What do you want?"

"Have you seen our friend, Mrs. Sheridan?" Karen

asked politely. "Has she come back?"

Belinda rolled her eyes. "How should I know? If you can't find your friend, you should call the police. It's not my job to track down your friends."

Karen and Meghan walked away, both disheartened. "I don't want to call the police," Meghan moaned. "They were so nasty when I was at the jail."

"I think you're going to have to do it," Karen told her. "Mrs. Sheridan has been missing for a while, and we don't want anything to happen to her. I think we need the police's help."

Meghan sighed. "Alright, alright," she said. "I'll go to the station; that would probably be better than calling; I need to ask Officer Brady a few questions about my case, anyway."

Karen yawned. "I'm going to go upstairs and go to sleep, but I will leave my phone on. Call me if you need *anything*."

About forty-five minutes later, Meghan arrived at the station. She approached the front desk and asked to speak with Officer Brady. When he came to get her, he had a surprised look on his face. "I didn't expect to see you here," he told her as he led her to his office.

"What's up?" he asked as he sat down at his desk. "Questions about your case? You must be an early bird; it's six in the morning…"

Meghan shook her head. "I need to report a missing

person," she informed him. "My friend, Sally Sheridan, is missing."

"How long has she been missing?"

"Awhile," she told him. "More than a day."

He stared at her. "Your friend has been missing more than a day and this is the first I'm hearing of this?" he asked incredulously. "This is Sin City; people go missing and get murdered all the time. This isn't your little Sandy Bay, Meghan. You have to ask for help as soon as something happens around here."

She glared at him. "How would I know that?" she spat. "I'm not from here. I am trying my best to help my friend."

He narrowed his eyes at her. "Miss Truman, this is a dangerous city," he said condescendingly. "Especially in the last month. We've had ten people go missing and five murders in the last thirty days. We wonder if we have a serial killer on the loose. Like I said, this isn't your sweet small town!"

Her lip quivered. "You don't have to talk to me like that," she murmured. "You don't have to be rude."

He shrugged. "I am just sick and tired of you tourists marching into town, causing trouble, and then flying home without a care in the world. You leave us police officers to pick up the pieces of your messes; whether we're finding your stolen wallets, or tracking down your missing friends, or calling your fancy banks because a scammer stole your credit cards at the casinos, we have to do the dirty work."

Meghan stood up. "I lost my credit and debit cards on the day we first stepped into this station. Has anyone handed them over?"

"Oh! Another stolen credit card case. No, I'm sorry Miss Truman, your missing credit cards have not been reported. Is there anything else you'd like to report?" he said, folding his hands across his chest.

"I'm sorry you feel that way," she said stoically, willing herself not to cry. "I'll get out of your hair now."

She left the police station and walked back to the hotel. She was overcome with frustration; Officer Brady was so rude and bitter, and she could not believe how unprofessional his outburst had been. She ached for Jack and the kind-hearted officers in Sandy Bay, and she hoped that she would be home sooner rather than later.

As she approached the hotel, her heart sank; police tape was wrapped around the parking lot, and two squad cars were parked out front. An ambulance pulled up with its siren wailing, and Meghan began to run toward the scene.

"What happened?" she asked an officer.

"Ma'am, if you are a guest here, you need to go inside. If you are not, you need to move along."

She shook her head. "I'm a guest, but so are my friends and sister. What happened? Is everyone okay?"

The officer shook his head. "There was an accident,"

he told her in a low voice. "An elderly woman was hit by a car."

"What?" she shrieked.

He nodded. "She was walking along with her cane, and the car drove right into her. It seemed intentional, if you ask me. We reviewed the footage, and it doesn't look like an accident. That poor old lady. She couldn't get out of the way in time."

Meghan wanted to vomit; it sounded like Mrs. Sheridan had been hit by the car! "Where was the victim taken?"

The officer gave her the information, and she hailed a taxi. "Valley Hospital Medical Center," she told the driver.

She could barely breathe as she was driven to the hospital. Had the collision been an accident? Who would try to hurt Mrs. Sheridan?

She arrived at the hospital and ran to the lobby. A receptionist greeted her warmly. "Can I help you?"

"I'm looking for the victim of the hit and run," she breathed worriedly. "Is she here? I'm family."

He nodded and directed her down the hallway. Meghan slowly walked down the dark corridor as her heart was beating frantically in her chest.

When she reached the door, she threw it open. She could see a silhouette of Mrs. Sheridan, and her stomach churned as she noticed the IVs connected to

her still body. She heard the buzz of the machines whirling, and she cringed; she couldn't bear to see Mrs. Sheridan in such terrible condition.

"Mrs. Sheridan," she wailed. "It's Meghan Truman! I'm here. Are you okay? I am so sorry for what happened to you. I can't believe it. Please be okay."

She hung her head, thinking of every negative thing she had ever said or thought about Mrs. Sheridan. "I'm sorry," she whimpered as she made her way to the bedside.

"You are the most amazing, wonderful woman in the world," Meghan wept. "I love you, and I hope you are okay."

Mrs. Sheridan grunted. "Go on."

"And you are fierce and funny and everyone in town just loves you!" Meghan assured her. "You are the best thing to happen to our town."

She pulled back the curtain that was hanging around the bed and gasped; the woman in the hospital bed was not Mrs. Sheridan.

"Oh, I am so sorry," she apologized as the woman peered curiously at her. "Forgive me for intruding. I will get out of your way."

The woman groaned, and Meghan clasped her hand over her mouth. "I am so sorry to bother you," she told her. "I didn't mean to intrude."

Filled with relief that the woman was not her friend, she was glad Mrs. Sheridan had not been the victim of a hit and run; however, she felt terrible for interrupting the poor woman.

"You can go on," the woman grunted. "With your compliments."

The woman shook her head. She pointed at Meghan. "Wait," she whispered as Meghan walked out of the room. "Come back. I want to talk with you…."

Not hearing the woman, Meghan left the hospital.

20

Meghan took a taxi back to the hotel. While she was tired and disheartened at not having located Mrs. Sheridan, she was grateful that Mrs. Sheridan was not the victim of the hit and run.

Lucky Elway greeted her as she walked into the lobby. “Why the long face? The Queen of the hotel should be smiling when she comes back to her castle.”

She tried to fake a smile, but she was unsuccessful. “Hey,” she said flatly.

“What’s the matter?”

She hung her head. “My friend is still missing,” she informed him. “Mrs. Sheridan? She’s the elderly woman with our group.”

He nodded. “I’ve heard about that,” he assured her. “And I am doing everything to help; I have a brother on the police force, and I’ve let him know about the situation. We will do our best to find your friend. Now, I must admit, there have been a lot of people who have gone missing in Las Vegas lately, so I’m going to do my best to make sure we find your friend.”

She smiled weakly. “Thank you,” she told him. “I appreciate the help. Mrs. Sheridan is a bit... zany... and I wouldn’t want anything to happen to her.”

Lucky wrinkled his nose. “Is there any possibility she could have met someone here?”

“Met someone?”

“Romantically? Maybe she met someone special and decided to elope? Plenty of people do it…”

She laughed. “That is absolutely not the case,” she promised him. “Mrs. Sheridan has her own romance drama back home.”

He raised an eyebrow. “You just never know…”

She shrugged. “What are you doing here, anyway? Here to upgrade me again?” she joked.

“Not quite,” he told her. “To celebrate our new place on the tourism board’s list of must-see Vegas locations, I wanted to treat you and your friends to an afternoon on the town. Myrtle mentioned that you haven’t had the best time here, and I want to change that. You've done a lot for my business, and I want to give back."

Her dark eyes widened. "That's kind of you. What do you have in mind?"

"I've rented a limo," he declared. "A stretch limo with a mini-bar inside. I want to take you ladies to The Venetian theater to see the new Elvis perform."

Meghan's body grew hot with discomfort. "I don't think that's a good idea," she dismissed. "I've had enough trouble there, and I don't want to bring any more attention to myself."

He shook his head. "Are you sure? It could be fun!"

Meghan's friends and sister appeared in the lobby. They were all dressed in cute outfits, and they seemed excited. "You're back!" Karen exclaimed. "Right on time, too. When we got your text that the woman was not Mrs. Sheridan, we were so pleased, and then Lucky showed up and invited us to the show!"

Myrtle nodded. "It'll be a fun time, Meghan. We should do it."

Meghan bit her lip. "Do you guys feel comfortable going out on the town without Mrs. Sheridan? I'm worried about her."

Trudy placed a hand on her shoulder. "Meghan, my dear," she began. "Sally is a grown woman. She has been taking care of herself longer than you've been alive. Don't worry about her. This is your party. We need to have some fun!"

Meghan wasn't sure, but seeing the eagerness on her friends' faces, she agreed. She quickly asked to be excused while she went up to her room to freshen up.

When she got back to the lobby, Lucky led them to the limo, and Jackie began pouring champagne into crystal flutes for each woman. "This is the life!" she shrieked as she popped her head out of the sunroof. "Cheers, girls!"

"Cheers!" Trudy toasted Jackie.

They offered a drink to Karen, but she refused. "I am training for a triathlon," she politely declined. "But that means more for Meghan!"

Meghan shook her head, but Myrtle talked her into drinking two of the flutes. "Come on, sis," Myrtle urged. "How often do you get to ride around Vegas in a limo? Live a little!"

Meghan half-heartedly agreed, but she had to admit, after drinking one of the flutes, she felt a lot more relaxed. Her exhaustion melted away, and she began to loosen up, singing along with the radio as Jackie selected a station, and toasting with all of her friends.

"Look!" Trudy cried as she pointed out the window. "The Eiffel Tower!"

Meghan could feel the sensation of her drinks, and she happily stuck her head out the window. "Wooo!" she cried. "This must be what Vegas is all about!"

Karen laughed as Meghan sat back down. "I'm glad you're finally enjoying yourself, sweetie," she

whispered as Meghan giggled. "Seems like we should have given you some champagne when we got on the airplane on the way here!"

They arrived at The Venetian, and Meghan felt very grand as she marched into the lobby. Several tourists took photos of her, but with the buzz from her drinks still about her, she did not care; she posed for photos, blowing kisses at the camera as though she were a proper celebrity.

"Hey! Meghan! Girls!"

The ladies smiled as Todd came up to them. "What are you up to?" Meghan asked sweetly. "It's so good to see you?"

She could see Jackie was glaring daggers at her; Meghan knew Jackie had a crush on Todd, but with the tingles of her champagne still tickling her mind and body, Meghan was feeling a little flirty and a little vindictive. "Todd, you look nice today," she cooed, feeling Jackie's eyes on her.

"I'm here to see the show," he told her, taking her hand and kissing it gently. "So good to see you ladies. Shall we go backstage and say hello to Earl? He invited me to see him, and I'm sure he'd love to see all of you."

"Let's do it," Meghan murmured as she batted her eyelashes at him.

Todd led them backstage to Earl's dressing room. Earl answered, but he did not appear happy to see

them. "Do you have an appointment?" he asked as he took a bite of a turkey sandwich.

"Earl, it's us, your friends," Meghan said. "We wanted to say hello!"

Earl looked down at his wrist. "I don't have time. I am on in a few minutes. You'll have to schedule something later with my assistant."

He slammed the door in their faces. "He wasn't even wearing a watch!" Meghan exclaimed. "What just happened?"

Todd shook his head. "Fame can really get to someone's head," he explained. "Some people return to normal after a few months, but others can get really into themselves."

"That's a shame," Myrtle commented.

Todd looked down at his watch. "Let's go find our seats. The show is going to start soon!"

They took their seats, and the lights came on. They saw Earl strut onto the stage holding a silver electric guitar. "Good evening, guys and dolls," he greeted. "Let's have a round of applause because the KING IS HERE!"

The audience applauded, and Earl began his set. "Wise men say...." he sang as he opened with a ballad.

He finished the song, and the group cheered. “He has a nice voice,” Karen murmured. “Even better than

Jeremiah’s!”

Meghan nodded. “It doesn’t sound like the real Elvis, but I really like it!”

He began to strum the guitar, but he stopped. He clutched his throat, and then his hands moved to his stomach. He began to retch, and the gasping sounds were alarming.

“What is going on?” Trudy asked in alarm. “Is he choking?”

Meghan recalled the turkey sandwich he had been eating when they tried to say hello. “It doesn’t look like he’s choking, but something looks wrong. I wonder if he’s having a reaction to that sandwich or something?”

Earl’s face went white, and before anything could be done, the lights went out. The entire theater was pitch-black, and all Meghan could hear were the sounds of the audience’s screams.

21

"Everyone, grab hands!" Meghan cried as her group stood from their seats in the darkness. "Karen, use your cell phone as a flashlight. Let's follow the emergency signs and get out of here!"

Their group slowly made their way out of the theater and back to the opulent lobby of The Venetian.

"Where's Todd?" Jackie asked worriedly. "I don't want to leave him behind!"

Todd had been seated in another section, and Meghan was not concerned. "He's fine," she told Jackie. "He can fend for himself. He knows Vegas better than we do, and I know he'll be fine."

A fire alarm started to go off. "What is happening?" Trudy said.

"Let's get back to the hotel," Meghan said quietly. They could still hear the screams from inside the theater. "We don't know what's going on, and we need to stay safe."

They went outside and hailed a taxi. Meghan's phone began to ring, and she excused herself from the group. "I'll be back," she mouthed to Karen.

"Babe!"

She smiled as she heard Jack's voice. "Hey."

"Are you okay?" he asked in alarm. "I didn't realize your trip had gone so crazy."

She frowned. "I called you and told you," she countered.

"You didn't tell me all of it! I googled your name, and it's CRAZY what's going on out there! You're in the middle of a murder investigation? Babe! I need to know those things. I could have helped sooner if I had known."

She sighed. "Babe, you didn't seem to take me seriously…"

"I am so sorry," he told her. "I didn't mean to be nonchalant; I should have taken you more seriously, and I am so sorry."

She was grateful to hear his apology. "Thanks, babe," she murmured.

"I called the police there," he told her. "I want to get you home as soon as possible, but…"

"But?"

"I spoke with an officer who doesn't seem to care for you."

"Officer Brady?"

"Yep," he confirmed. "It sounds like it's gonna be harder to get you home than I thought; that guy is a piece of work. I realized after we spoke that we've actually met before. He was my supervisor at a training course in Rhode Island a few summers ago. That guy was such a jerk."

"He's awful," she agreed. "What did he say about the case?"

"It doesn't matter," he said sadly. "But I don't think they're going to let me whisk you away. I thought if I spoke to him, one officer to another, that he would give in, but he isn't going to."

"UGHHH!" Meghan cried. "What am I going to have to do to get home?"

"I'm not sure yet," he admitted. "But if this isn't settled sooner than later, I am coming out there. I can't have a jailbird for a fiancé, and you belong with me at home!"

They said goodbye, and Meghan returned to her

group. They were jumping into a taxi, and they sped away from The Venetian.

When they returned to the hotel, Belinda sauntered up to Meghan. “Someone called for you,” she told her.

“Oh? Who?” Meghan asked. “Was it Mrs. Sheridan? Did she leave a message?”

“How should I know who is calling you?” Belinda asked rudely. “It’s not my job to take your messages.

“Did they leave a name? A return number?” Meghan asked.

“It was a woman’s voice, I think, but she didn’t leave a name.”

Meghan nodded. “Thanks. Hey, is Todd on duty later? Our group has really connected with him and we want to take him to dinner.”

She was bluffing, but she was irritated by Belinda’s rudeness and wanted her to feel slighted. Meghan wasn’t usually vindictive, but after several days of little rest and enormous stress, she could hardly control herself.

“No, he won’t. He’s at his second job right now.”

“Second job?”

Belinda raised an eyebrow. “You didn’t know? He’s an Elvis impersonator. That’s why he likes going to all the Elvis shows, and that’s why Jeremiah Wilson spent so much time here. They started working in the same group of Elvis actors."

Meghan's eyes widened. "I didn't know that about

him," she admitted. "Where does he perform?"

"He doesn't have a major gig," Belinda explained. "Did you notice that he can hardly move his hips? He had a hip replacement at a young age, and he can hardly move them. He can stand still, and he can walk just fine, but he can't dance like Elvis. That's why he never got a major gig. Everyone wants to see the King swing those hips."

Meghan nodded. "That makes sense, I guess."

She felt someone tap her on the shoulder. "Hey." It was Officer Brady.

"Hi," she greeted him coldly. "What do you need?"

He pointed at the women. "I need to get statements from all of you," he told her. "Standard procedure. Are you all available?"

Before she could reply, she saw Todd enter the lobby. "Hey!" she greeted him warmly. "Belinda said you were out tonight. She told us about your second job. That is so cool!"

Todd's eyes grew large when he saw Officer Brady standing next to Meghan. "I have to go," he muttered, and he turned on his heel and ran away.

“Todd? Are you okay?” Karen shouted after him.

“Todd? What’s the matter?” Jackie yelled.

Officer Brady turned away from Meghan and put his hand on the gun sitting in his belt. “Todd Sherman!

Come back here! Right now!”

Meghan’s jaw dropped as Officer Brady took off sprinting after Todd. Why was the officer who had been interrogating her chasing the manager of the hotel? Meghan had to find out. She ran after the two men, her friends trailing behind her.

22

As soon as Meghan stepped outside into the warm Vegas evening, she saw Officer Brady climb into his car and turn the lights on. "Wait!" she shouted as she ran to the passenger door. "I want to come with you."

He shook his head, but she threw herself inside. "What's going on?" she asked as they sped off.

"We have to catch that man," he told her as he navigated his car onto the Strip. "We have wanted to talk to him about the death of Jeremiah Wilson, and he has been uncooperative."

"You think he has something to do with Jeremiah's death?" she asked in alarm. "Todd? But he is so nice!"

Officer Brady swung the steering wheel left to avoid

hitting a tourist who was jaywalking. "I don't have all the information," he admitted. "But I do know that my boss wants to speak with that guy immediately."

He pressed down on the gas and the car sped forward. "There he is!" Meghan pointed out the window as she spotted Todd. "He's running across the street. I don't know if we'll be able to get over there."

"Oh, yes we will," Officer Brady assured her. He veered left, and then right, and they continued following Todd down the Strip.

"What if he goes into a store?" Meghan asked. "We'll lose him."

"We're getting closer and closer," Officer Brady mumbled as he kept his eyes focused on Todd. "Look, that guy can barely run."

"It's his hips," Meghan explained.

"How exactly do you know that?" he asked her as he raised an eyebrow.

"His co-worker told me!" she stated defensively. "It's not like I knew him well. Belinda, the other receptionist at our hotel, told us he had a hip replacement. That's why he could never get a major gig as an Elvis impersonator."

Officer Brady pursed his lips. "I'm gonna have to add that to his file. Interesting."

"Be careful!" Meghan cried as a teenager dashed

across the street. "Don't hit him."

"I'm a professional," he told her, turning to look at her as he passed two cars, narrowly avoiding hitting the teenager. "You need to calm down."

He steered down the block. "You're going to hit someone!" she screamed again as he missed colliding with a family. "You are a terrible driver!"

Officer Brady looked to the right. "He's getting away," he muttered. "We have to go faster!"

He hit the gas pedal and the car took off. Meghan had never moved so quickly in a vehicle, and she felt nauseated as they made a sharp left turn. "He's going in the other direction!" she cried as Officer Brady scowled.

"I am gaining momentum!" he shouted. "This is how you do it!"

Meghan buried her face in her hands. She was terrified as the car moved in and out of pedestrian traffic, and she was scared they would hit someone. "Someone would blame me for that, too," she thought as Officer Brady threw on the brakes.

"Why are you stopping?" she screamed.

He said nothing, and she watched as a mother pushing a stroller walked in front of the stopped car.

"Couldn't hit such a sweet little family," he told her with a grin on his face.

As soon as they passed, he threw the car back into motion; he clutched the steering wheel as he stomped

on the gas pedal. "Let's gooooo!"

He turned to look at Meghan. "What's your problem?" he asked with a look of disgust on his face. "I'm trying to catch him. Isn't that what you want?"

Before she could respond, the police car crashed into a pedestrian barrier. Meghan felt the impact of the airbags hitting her stomach, and she moaned as she jerked against her seatbelt. Officer Brady muttered some expletives, but he did not stop to assess his injuries. He leapt from the car and ran into the crowd of bystanders who had gathered to watch.

Meghan slowly untangled herself from the car. She could hear the wail of sirens growing closer, and an ambulance pulled up beside the mangled police car. She looked into the crowd, and before she lost consciousness, she saw Officer Brady putting a pair of handcuffs on Todd Sherman.

Three days later, Meghan and her friends were waiting in the security line at McCarran International Airport. Meghan had been released from the hospital the previous night; she had suffered from a minor concussion, but the doctors in Las Vegas assured her that she would be safe to fly home. Now, as she clutched her carry-on bags and waited to walk through the x-ray machine, she was happier than ever.

"We're finally going home!" she squealed to Myrtle as the line moved forward.

The police had instantly cleared Meghan and her friends after arresting Todd Sherman. Officer Brady

had visited Meghan at the hospital and told her the full story: it turned out that Todd had been Jeremiah's unofficial understudy in the show at The Venetian. Sometimes, when Jeremiah was tired or ill, Todd would take the stage for a song or two.

Todd wanted more than a few songs; he wanted his own show. He devised a plan to kill Jeremiah, and he had slipped an excessive number of sleeping pills into a drink he had served him earlier at the hotel. He thought if Jeremiah was dead, then he would be asked to do the show, but the producers and directors had disagreed and given the part to Earl, enjoying his younger look and admiring his vocal abilities.

Todd had been planning to kill Earl too, but his plan had not worked; he had not been able to put enough sleeping pills in Earl's drink to kill him, and while Earl was still recovering, he would be up and moving in a few days.

Meghan was flabbergasted. "But Jeremiah and Todd were friends," she said as Officer Brady finished his explanation.

"Not quite," he told her. "Todd told us that Jeremiah used to make fun of him about his bad hips, and it sounds like it really got to the guy. Todd started to hate Jeremiah, and their friendship was ruined."

Meghan was overjoyed when Officer Brady handed her the debit and credit cards she had lost and almost forgotten about. Her Las Vegas trip had been such a rollercoaster of mishaps, that she had forgotten about them. Apparently, the officer who had booked them, had placed them in a wrong file.

Now, at the airport, with her name cleared, Meghan felt so much better; her head still ached, and she was still tired, but she was finally on her way home.

"Meghan, look!" Karen said as she pointed to a big-screen television tucked in the corner. It was showing a local news broadcast, and Meghan's image appeared on the screen with the word INNOCENT under her photo.

"About time I get some good press," she joked as the ladies chuckled.

The news report continued, and they saw Louise's face appear. "Mrs. Wilson, the ex-wife of the deceased Jeremiah Wilson, has been extradited to Cincinnati," a blonde reporter announced. "She will be tried for the murder of her previous ex-husband," the reporter stated.

"Ugh, that woman," Meghan muttered. "I'm glad I'll never have to deal with her again."

The report moved to a video clip of Louise's attorney being brought into a courtroom. "And her attorney was officially disbarred after it was found that they were fraternizing inappropriately," the report continued.

"That guy was so gross," Karen commented as the

reporter moved on. "I'm glad he is getting what he deserves. That kind of person shouldn't be a lawyer."

Jackie smiled. "It all worked out well after all!" she

chirped merrily. "And my cousin texted me. Meghan, you remember her? The one from jail?"

Meghan resisted the urge to roll her eyes.

"She's being transferred from jail to rehab. She filed an appeal, and her lawyer recommended that she would be better suited in a rehab facility. She's going to get the help she needs."

"That's nice," Meghan said, trying her best to be gracious.

"She'll be out in time for your wedding!" Jackie cried. "You two really hit it off, so I'm so glad she'll be able to make it."

Myrtle wrinkled her nose. "The guest list hasn't been finalized," she began, but Meghan cut her off.

"Just let it be," she whispered to her sister. "Just let it be for now."

Although everything seemed to have returned to normal, there was something still playing on Meghan's mind. Mrs. Sheridan still hadn't been found. Meghan was reluctant to leave Las Vegas until she was found but Officer Brady had assured her that her type of disappearance was something the police dealt with all the time. What would she tell Frank if she bumped into him? She had relayed her concerns to Jack and he had been in touch with the Las Vegas law enforcement team.

Suddenly, they all heard a buzzing sound. “Did all of our phones just go off at the same time?” Trudy asked as they all retrieved their phones from their pockets.

“I’m fine,” they all said in unison as they read the text.

“Who is it from?” Karen asked.

“I don’t have this number,” Jackie commented.

“Neither do I,” Meghan said. “But I hope it’s Mrs. Sheridan. She *still* hasn’t been found…”

23

"Surprise!"

Two weeks after returning home from Las Vegas, Karen had insisted that she pick Meghan up after work and take her to dinner. Meghan agreed, eager to visit with her friend, and she happily climbed into Karen's jeep after closing up the bakery.

"Where are we going? That new health food place?" Meghan asked.

"Nope," Karen said with a glimmer in her eye. "It's a secret."

Karen drove her to the event barn Meghan and Jackie owned. "What are we doing here?" Meghan asked. "We don't have food here."

"Just come with me!" Karen commanded, and she took Meghan's hand and led her inside.

When she threw open the doors, Meghan was shocked to find Myrtle, Pamela, Trudy, Jackie, and Mrs. Sheridan waiting for her. "Surprise!"

The barn was decorated with pink tablecloths, pink balloons, streamers, and a cake. "What is going on?" she asked in amazement. "Mrs. Sheridan! You're here! You're okay!"

Mrs. Sheridan embraced her. "Sorry to scare you," she apologized. "But I had to make it back for your bachelorette party!"

"My bachelorette party?" Meghan asked. "What? We already had it in Vegas!"

Jackie shook her head. "We wanted to make it up to you," she said softly. "I know your party was a bust, and we wanted to give you a bachelorette party you would really enjoy."

"This is incredible!" Meghan cried as she embraced Jackie. "I can't believe this!"

Jackie's eyes widened. "Do you like it?"

"I love it!" Meghan assured her. "A quiet girls' night with my favorite girls? I feel sooo lucky!"

Karen laughed. "I'm glad it was a surprise," she said happily. "We were afraid we would give away the secret."

"I was afraid *I* wouldn't be able to keep the secret,"

Mrs. Sheridan squawked. "Do you want to know where I've been?"

"Yes!" Meghan exclaimed. "I was worried about you!"

Mrs. Sheridan pulled up her sleeve and revealed a large diamond on her left hand. "I got married in Las Vegas!"

"Married?" Meghan screeched. "To who?"

"To Frank, silly!" Mrs. Sheridan laughed. "I missed him terribly, and I felt bad that we quarreled before I left. I called him up and invited him to Vegas. We got married at the Graceland Wedding Chapel! Elvis married us!"

Meghan shook her head. "I can't believe you were in Vegas the whole time."

"I wasn't," Mrs. Sheridan told her. "We were married, and then we left for our honeymoon in Phoenix. We flew out that day, and we just got back yesterday."

Meghan shook her head. "Why didn't you tell anyone? We were so worried."

Mrs. Sheridan shrugged. "I didn't think you would worry," she admitted. "I'm a grown woman and can take care of myself. I've been taking care of myself longer than you've all been alive!"

Meghan giggled. "Well, let me give a toast, then!" she declared. "All of my favorite ladies are here to

celebrate with me, and I want to give a toast!"

Jackie popped open a bottle of champagne and passed out pink plastic flutes that had Meghan and Jack's initials intertwined inside of a heart.

"I'd like to give a toast to my dear friends!" Meghan announced. "To all of my girls who went to Vegas, and who support me in my business, and who got together to put this party together. I love you all, and I can't wait to walk into the next phase of my life with all of my ladies by my side."

She saw Karen dab her eyes with a handkerchief.

"You are all the best friends I could ever ask for," she told them. "I am so grateful for you! Thank you for all you've done for me. I am so lucky to be marrying the best man in the world, Jack. I am so lucky to have a job I love in a town I am devoted to. And last but not least, I am so grateful to have you as my friends! Having friends like you is *truly* sweet!"

The End

Afterword

Thank you for reading Rhubarb Pie and Revenge! I really hope you enjoyed reading it as much as I had writing it!

If you have a minute, please consider leaving a review on Amazon, GoodReads and/or Bookbub.

Many thanks in advance for your support!

About Peaches and Crime

Released: April, 2019
Series: Book 12 – Sandy Bay Cozy Mystery Series

A suspicious fatal accident. A murder case going cold. Can a small town bakery owner overcome her personal problems and find a happy ending?

Running one business can be stressful. Running two is murder! Meghan's new, yummy peach dessert range is evoking pleasant noises from her customers, including the Governor of the state. Her sense of euphoria at creating another culinary winner is cut short when she discovers that the premises of her other business, an event barn, has been vandalized.

The rude and obnoxious behavior of an alleged expert, called in to beef up the security at The Barn, gives Meghan grief and concern. When this person is found dead on her business premises, her heart breaks for the person's loved ones.

Could this death be accidental or intentional?

Meghan finds herself at a crossroad as she has to make decisions that could have lasting consequences.

The security of her customers' needs to be guaranteed but at what cost?...

Her long-term relationship with her boyfriend has hit the rocks and seems irreparable...

Will Meghan help to find a killer still on the loose or see everything she's worked so hard to build, come crashing down?

PEACHES AND CRIME CHAPTER 1 SNEEK PEEK

Meghan Truman sighed contentedly as she leaned against the goose feather down comforter on the king bed in her hotel room. She was exhausted from a long day; she had woke up at four in the morning to travel to Seattle. Upon arrival at the hotel, she had dropped off her bags and dashed off to the first breakout session of the Women in Business Fellowship Conference she had decided to attend on a whim. Now, only moments after the final session of the day, she could finally relax.

She peered around the room as she settled into the bed. The hotel room was twice the size of her apartment, and the dark wood finishing and antique furniture made Meghan feel elegant. The lights were low, but she was fine with that; she needed time to rest and process what had been a nearly eighteen hour day.

"Ahhh," she breathed happily as she pulled a beige wool throw blanket over her lap. "This is the nicest hotel I've ever stayed in. I wish my apartment were as nice as this place!"

She heard a knock at her door. “Meghan? It’s me. Open up!”

She groaned, rising from the bed and padding to the heavy oak door. “Kirsty? I don’t want to go to the happy hour. I’m ready for bed.”

Meghan opened the door to find Kirsty Fisher standing before her, her hands on her hips. “I’m telling you, Meghan, you’ll regret it if you don’t go,” she lectured, her eyebrows raised. “The breakout sessions are fine, but the social events is where the real learning happens at this conference.”

Meghan folded her arms over her chest, resisting the urge to roll her eyes. Kirsty was one of the first people Meghan had met in Sandy Bay, her adopted hometown. She was a few years older than Meghan, and she had taken Meghan under her wing in her own sort of way. Kirsty was a wildly successful entrepreneur, and while she was still bouncing back from a nasty divorce, her latest business venture, a boutique event planning service, was launching soon, and it had received attention in the local and state press.

“I invited you to this conference for a reason,” Kirsty went on, the hallway lights making her blonde bob seem even brighter. “This is an opportunity for you to learn how to grow your business and provide customers with unforgettable experiences. I’ve never invited anyone to this event before, but I thought you would be the perfect person. I am hoping I wasn’t wrong…”

Meghan's heart sank. She *was* grateful that Kirsty had invited her to the conference; Meghan's business, a thriving bakery that had recently celebrated its one year anniversary, was growing rapidly, and she wanted to develop herself more as a professional. She had been eager to attend the conference, but now, as she stood in her pajamas, the last thing she wanted to do was network in the hotel lounge.

"Fine," Kirsty said, snapping her bubble-gum pink lips. "I can tell that you aren't interested. I'll just go by myself. It's a pity, really…"

"Give me five minutes," Meghan grumbled. "I need to put on a clean outfit and run a brush through my hair."

Kirsty's face brightened. "That's the spirit," she commended. "Here, let me help you choose an outfit. You have a white leather skirt, yes?"

Fifteen minutes later, Meghan and Kirsty sauntered into the hotel lounge. Meghan was dressed just like Kirsty; both women wore all-white ensembles, and while Meghan's style was typically casual, she was enjoying being dressed to the nines.

"You look fabulous," Kirsty complimented as Meghan blushed. "That skirt and the white turtleneck look sharp. It really complements your skin tone."

Meghan smiled as they sat down at a tall black table. She tucked her long, wavy hair behind her ears and peered at the menu. "What should I order?" she whispered. "It's been forever since I've been out, and I don't think I've ever been out at such a chic place..."

Kirsty winked. "I'll order the drinks. You have a bit of eyeliner on your cheek; why don't you run to the ladies room and get it off?"

Meghan's dark eyes widened. "Whoops," she lamented as she rose from the table. "I'll be right back."

When Meghan returned to the table, she saw Kirsty was sitting with two other women. "The keynote speakers," Meghan murmured as she recognized them. "Kirsty knows the keynote speakers?"

"Meghan," Kirsty greeted her as she sat down. "Ladies, this is my dear friend, Meghan Truman. Meghan is a business owner in Sandy Bay. She owns a bakery, and she is self-taught! This girl never even went to culinary school, and she managed to turn a profit last year. She has had a wonderful year of learning the business, and she is excited to learn more through our time together at the conference."

The woman to Kirsty's left nodded warmly. She appeared to be in her mid-forties, and she was a statuesque beauty. She had long, black braids trailing down her back, and her skin was the color of a mocha latte.

"It's a pleasure to meet you," she said as she reached to shake Meghan's hand. Her grip was firm and her smile was sincere. "I'm Kyrayah Glint. It's always a treat to meet young business women."

"The pleasure is mine," Meghan replied. "I loved your talk this afternoon. Your discussion on your experiences operating a non-profit in Somalia was eye-opening."

Kyrayah's smile widened. "I'm happy to hear that. I grew up in Kenya, which neighbors Somalia, and the work I do in east Africa is near and dear to my heart."

Kirsty gestured to the other woman, a thin, pale woman with raven hair pulled tight into a bun atop her head. "And this is Jacqueline, Meghan. She owns and operates a beauty empire in the Midwest."

"An empire? That is exciting!"

Jacqueline scowled. "It's busy, to say the least," she said, eyeing Meghan's messy hair. "So, you're a cook?"

"I own a bakery," Meghan politely corrected. "In Sandy Bay."

"That's lovely," Kyrayah cooed. "And what perfect timing to talk about a bakery; I spy a waiter with desserts. Let's flag him down!"

Kirsty waved over a uniformed waiter holding a platter of delicacies. "I shouldn't," she said as he placed down three small plates in front of the four women. "I'm really trying to stick to keto…"

"Forget keto," Kyrayah urged her. "You are with the ladies tonight! Have some treats with your fellow boss babes, Kirsty."

Kirsty smiled. "Only if Jacqueline will."

Jacqueline frowned. "You know I don't do sugar," she chided. "Morgan can have my dessert."

"It's Meghan," she softly interjected. "Meghan."

"Whatever," Jacqueline replied. "Here, take this. It looks like a peach tart."

"Let's all taste them together," Kyrayah declared. "It will be more fun. One, two, three!"

Kirsty, Meghan, and Kyrayah each took a small bite of the peach tarts. "This is HEAVENLY!" Kirsty exclaimed.

"This is the best thing I have ever tasted," Kyrayah agreed. "Meghan? What do you think? You are the baking expert."

She licked her lips. "It's incredible," she agreed. "I need to start looking into making some peach desserts! I feel inspired."

Kirsty laughed and playfully swatted Meghan on the shoulder. "You couldn't possibly make something this good," she teased as Meghan's eyes widened. "This dessert was made by angels or something."

"Oh, come on," Meghan replied good-naturedly. "I know I could come up with a good peach dessert. What if I made a honey bourbon cream to pour on top of it? Bourbon and peaches are a match made in Heaven."

"I don't know," Kirsty said. "I think a dessert of this caliber might be out of your reach, dear. Not to hurt your feelings, but it's important to get critical feedback from like-minded women. Right, ladies?"

Jacqueline and Kyrayah nodded. "Feedback is crucial," Jacqueline agreed. "It's how you get better."

"Maybe with some more training, you could make desserts like this," Kyrayah suggested kindly. "Perhaps a cooking class or two?"

Meghan's smile faded. Kirsty's silly jab had quickly offended her, and now she was suggesting to two of the most important, influential women Meghan had ever met that her desserts were lackluster. She struggled to remain composed as the ladies continued to chat.

"Meghan? You look upset," Kirsty noticed. "I was only teasing about the desserts. I'm sure you can make a fine peach tart."

"Of course," she muttered as she stared down at her shoes. "Only teasing. No worries, Kirsty. No worries at all."

-

You can order your copy of **Peaches and Crime** at any good online retailer.

A SANDY BAY 16 COZY MYSTERY
Peaches
and
Crime
AMBER CREWES

ALSO BY AMBER CREWES

The Sandy Bay Cozy Mystery Series

Apple Pie and Trouble

Brownies and Dark Shadows

Cookies and Buried Secrets

Donuts and Disaster

Éclairs and Lethal Layers

Finger Foods and Missing Legs

Gingerbread and Scary Endings

Hot Chocolate and Cold Bodies

Ice Cream and Guilty Pleasures

Jingle Bells and Deadly Smells

King Cake and Grave Mistakes

Lemon Tarts and Fiery Darts

Muffins and Coffins

Nuts and a Choking Corpse

Orange Mousse and a Fatal Truce

Newsletter Signup

Want **FREE** COPIES OF FUTURE **AMBER CREWES** BOOKS, FIRST NOTIFICATION OF NEW RELEASES, CONTESTS AND GIVEAWAYS?

GO TO THE LINK BELOW TO SIGN UP TO THE NEWSLETTER!

www.AmberCrewes.com/cozylist

Printed in the USA
CPSIA information can be obtained
at www.ICGtesting.com
LVHW091242140724
785421LV00029B/291